William Shakespeare's

Romeo *and* Juliet

TEACHER'S RESOURCE BOOK

Philip Page and Marilyn Pettit

ILLUSTRATED BY
Philip Page

Published in association with

Hodder & Stoughton
A MEMBER OF THE HODDER HEADLINE GROUP

Acknowledgements
The publisher would like to thank the following copyright holders for permission to reproduce their photographs:
Page 21 © Donald Cooper, Photostage
Page 28 Ronald Grant Archive
Page 12 Ronald Grant Archive/© Twentieth Century Fox
Page 23 Alastair Muir
Pages 16, 19 and 42 The Moviestore Collection

Every effort has been made to trace copyright holders of material reproduced in this book. Any rights not acknowledged here will be acknowledged in subsequent printings if notice is given to the publisher.

Orders: please contact Bookpoint Ltd, 39 Milton Park, Abingdon, Oxon OX14 4TD. Telephone: (44) 01235 400414, Fax: (44) 01235 400454. Lines are open from 9.00–6.00, Monday to Saturday, with a 24 hour message answering service.
Email address: orders@bookpoint.co.uk

British Library Cataloguing in Publication Data
A catalogue record for this title is available from The British Library

ISBN 0 340 74300 X

First published 1999
Impression number   10 9 8 7 6 5 4 3 2
Year   2005 2004 2003 2002 2001 2000 1999

Copyright © 1999 Philip Page and Marilyn Pettit
Illustrations © 1999 Philip Page

All rights reserved. No part of this publication may be reproduced or transmitted in any form or by any means, electronic or mechanical, including photocopy, recording, or any information storage and retrieval system, without permission in writing from the publisher or under licence from the Copyright Licensing Agency Limited. Further details of such licences (for reprographic reproduction) may be obtained from the Copyright Licensing Agency Limited, of 90 Tottenham Court Road, London W1P 9HE.

Cover illustration by Lee Stinton
Typeset by Fakenham Photosetting Ltd, Fakenham, Norfolk
Printed in Great Britain for Hodder & Stoughton Educational, a division of Hodder Headline Plc, 338 Euston Road, London NW1 3BH by Hobbs the Printers, Totton, Hampshire.

Contents

Introduction — v

Introductory activities
Fact or opinion? Who was Shakespeare? — 1
Can you judge a book by its cover? — 2
An interview with an Elizabethan theatre goer 1 — 3
An interview with an Elizabethan theatre goer 2 — 4

Activities for Act 1
You've spoilt it for me! It's not worth watching now! — 5
Actions speak louder than words — 6
You'll never guess what he said! — 7
In love with love! — 8
Writing a missing scene — 9
Invitations and masks — 10
In the meantime — 11
Love at first sight! — 12

Activities for Act 2
Sunday ... Monday ... — 13
Do you think I am doing the right thing? — 14
Sticks and stones may break my bones, but names will never hurt me! — 15
What's in a name? — 16
I challenge you ... — 17
Crack the code! — 18
A friend in need ... is a friend indeed — 19
The first sign of madness — 20
In a minute, in a minute! — 21
Party dresses/wedding dresses — 22

Activities for Act 3
It had to happen – the turning point! — 23
Television brings you up-to-date news — 24
Banished ... — 25
There are two sides to every story — 26
What is she trying to say? — 27

I don't believe this has happened	28
Writing a letter of despair	29
You've got a lot to be thankful for!	30
What's the plan? – another missing scene	31
Parting is such sweet sorrow!	32
The story so far	33
Parents!	34
Continue the scene ...	35

Activities for Act 4

A desperate plan!	36
Sending a telegram	37
What are they thinking now?	38
Good news!	39
Juliet's worries	40
Thought tracking	41

Activities for Act 5

A letter explaining everything	42
Just a note to say that ...	43
What Balthasar saw	44
Stop right there! Don't do it!	45
The story is over ...	46

After the play activities

Stop! Cut the action!	47
Here lies the body of ... 1	48
Here lies the body of ... 2	49
Read all about it!	50
Come and see the play: the greatest love story ever told!	51
Sort out the jumble!	52
Writing horoscopes	53
Good evening and welcome!	54
If only ...	55
Who is to blame?	56
So you want to be a star?	57
Time waits for no man!	58

Answers 59

Introduction

The worksheets in this Teacher's Resource Book are intended to be used with *Livewire Shakespeare: Romeo and Juliet Pupil's Book.* All references, such as page numbers, relate to that book.

The worksheets address the pupils directly, so that, where appropriate, there is opportunity for pupil autonomy. However, the majority of the tasks lend themselves to teacher/pupil/class interaction.

They attempt to provide a background to Shakespeare and his theatre, so that the play can be viewed as a *stage play*, rather than a text. This approach is continued throughout the book.

All four language modes: Speaking, Listening, Reading and Writing are considered in the tasks.

There are a variety of activities, so that pupils experience: collaborative and individual work; a wide range of written pieces; drama pieces; and debate and discussion with reference to both Shakespearean language and today's English.

The activities have been devised with the SATs and the 'teenage classroom' in mind.

Together with the development of an understanding of Shakespeare, the emphasis is on fun, where pupils learn to support and evaluate their work.

Introductory activities

Fact or opinion?
Who was Shakespeare?

We can be sure of **facts**, but we can't be sure of **opinions**.

Opinions are what some people think or believe are true, but no-one can be sure that they are right.

Facts are true, and we can prove it!

Try to sort out the FACTS from the OPINIONS in the following list about Shakespeare's life.

- We think that he was born in 1564.
- We know that he was baptised in Stratford-upon-Avon.
- We're not sure, but we think that he went to school in Stratford.
- Some people believe that he left school to help his father in his business.
- He got married in 1582 to Anne Hathaway.
- They had three children.
- We know he went to London.
- Some people say that he had to leave Stratford because he had stolen a deer!
- We are certain that he was an actor.
- We don't know for sure what theatre company he worked in.
- We know that he owned part of a theatre called The Globe.
- We know that he wrote lots of plays and poems.
- He died in 1616.
- He is buried in a church in Stratford.
- On his gravestone, there are words that put a curse on anyone who moves his body!

Introductory activities

Can you judge a book by its cover?

Can you tell what a book is going to be about, just by looking at the cover?
Let's look at the cover of *Romeo and Juliet*. We can see objects that might suggest ideas to us. These are called **symbols**.

1 Think about:
Swords: what do you think of? Write down some ideas and share them with a partner.

A rose: what does that suggest? Again, write down your ideas and share them with a partner.

A mask: who might wear that kind of mask and why? Share your written ideas with a partner.

2 What about the **colours** on the cover: RED and YELLOW.
What do you think of when you see these two colours? Talk about it with your partner.

3 Now that you've looked at the symbols and colours, see if you can guess something about the story of the play. Write down some ideas with a partner. Share these with the rest of the class.

Introductory activities

An interview with an Elizabethan theatre goer 1

Just imagine that you could talk to someone who had seen the very first Shakespeare plays.
You could learn a lot about the theatre without reading any books at all.
It would be **first hand experience**. That means it would not be what someone else had said. You'd be talking to the **real theatre goer**!

1 Look at the questions below. These are some that you might ask. The answers, on Sheet 2, are jumbled up. Match them up with the answers. Write your answers like this: 1D.

2 When you've matched up the questions and answers, try one of these:

– Design a board that an actor might carry to say that a play is set in London.
– Draw the flag that might be raised above the theatre if the play *Romeo and Juliet* is about to be performed.

Questions

1 How did you know when a play was about to begin?
2 When did a play usually take place?
3 How much did you pay to get in?
4 Did you have to stand in the pit all the time?
5 Was there any scenery?
6 What were the costumes like?
7 How did you know when a scene ended if there was no curtain?
8 How did you know what time of day it was in the play if it was daylight where you were standing?

(Continued on Sheet 2)

Introductory activities

An interview with an Elizabethan theatre goer 2

(Continued from Sheet 1)

Answers

A Well, a play had to take place in the daylight, usually at two o'clock. We didn't have lighting like you do, you know.

B The costumes were so beautiful. Once I saw a velvet cloak with silver and gold on it, that cost over £20! A sheep only cost 40p!

C With no curtain, you had to listen for two lines that rhymed – that's called a rhyming couplet – and when that was said and the actors left the stage, the scene had ended – easy!

D We all looked out for the flag above the theatre – that's how you knew a play was about to begin.

E Oh yes, we had to stand in the pit all the time. To tell the truth, we could walk about and leave for a bit if we were bored, but we always came back!

F We paid just a penny to get into the pit and stand around three sides of the stage. But, if we wanted a seat, we paid another penny. We kept dry then under the thatched roof. But it was still a bit smelly and noisy.

G Scenery? Oh yes, there were some things, like a few chairs, but mostly we had to listen carefully to know what was going on and where the play was set.

H To know if it was night or dawn or in the middle of the day, you just had to listen to what the actors said – if they talked about the moon it was night; if they talked about the sun in the sky, it was day. Simple!

Activities for Act 1

You've spoilt it for me! It's not worth watching now!

When have you heard people say that?
Usually it is when someone says, 'Did you see that film last night?' They go on to tell you what happened, even the end and YOU wanted to watch it on video!

Read the Chorus again on page 1 of the play.
Someone comes onto the stage and tells you the whole story AND how it's going to end! Nobody leaves, though.
Everybody stays to watch the play.
Why do you think people stay?

1 Imagine that you have to write the Chorus's words in **Standard English** – that is English understood by everyone living in Britain today.
Now write the story, using the ideas you have read in the Chorus.
You might start by saying:

There were two families who lived in Verona, and …

2 When you have finished, share your work with a partner. See if you used the same words in places. This is called **comparing** your work.
Talk about why you chose the same or similar words.
If you enjoy music, you might try **rapping** your story.

3 Now work in groups of four.
One of you will take the part of the Chorus and tell the story; the others will make **freeze frames** to show what happens in the play.
Freeze frames are like frozen pictures. You must show the class what happens by moving into positions and staying very still, until you can move into the next freeze frame.
What did your class think about your frames?

Activities for Act I

Actions speak louder than words

What you DO often says more about you than what you SAY.

With a partner think about times when something you do is very important. For example, holding a young child's hand to make them feel safe.

The characters on pages 2, 3 and 4 are:

- fighting
- insulting each other
- shouting!

But ... WORDS are also important.

1 Match the words below with the character.

2 Then, write down what you learn about each one. Who was most sensible?

> Part, fools, put up your swords. I do but keep the peace.

> I hate the word, as I hate hell, all Montagues, and thee.

> Hold me not. Let me go.

> A crutch, a crutch! Why call you for a sword?

> Give me my long sword, ho!

> Thou shalt not stir one foot to seek a foe.

> If ever you disturb our streets again your lives shall pay the forfeit of the peace.

Activities for Act 1

You'll never guess what he said!

How many times have you heard that said by someone?
What might they say next?
'Well I'm not telling you'
'Go and ask someone else'
'OK, listen and I'll tell you'
Of course, they'll say something like the last one!

1 Imagine that you have just seen the fight that took place between the Montagues and the Capulets. You also stopped to listen to what the Prince said when he arrived.
Now you are **reporting** the speech to a friend.
You need to read the words spoken by the Prince on page 4 and then try to put them into your own words as much as possible.
You might think about the following to help you:

- Could the Prince be heard over the noise when he first arrived?
- What does he tell them to do with their weapons?
- Does he talk to Capulet and Montague?
- What does he say will happen to the two old men, if there are more fights?
- When does he want to see the two men?

You might begin to **report** what you heard like this:

Well, I just happened to be passing when I heard all this noise, and our Prince was there shouting ...

2 When you have written down what you want to say, practise it in front of a partner. Listen to your partner's piece as well.
You might also make your report in front of the class. Listen to other pupils' ideas about it.
When you do this, you are **evaluating**.
Listening to others helps you to improve.

Activities for Act I

In love with love!

In some of Shakespeare's plays, people who are in love act in a particular way. It's almost as if there were RULES about how to act if you were in love.

Think about today – are there ways in which people behave if they are in love? For example, pop singers sing about being happy together, holding hands, laughing together, never wanting to say goodbye.
Can you think of other things?

Let's turn to Romeo – was he really in love with Rosaline? When Romeo *thought* he was in love with Rosaline, he acted in a certain way. He was **in love with love**!

Look at pages 4 and 5. Try to describe how Romeo was behaving when he said he was in love with Rosaline. These lines spoken by Benvolio will help you:

So early walking did I see your son
Towards him I made, but he was ware of me,
And stole into the covert of the wood.

These lines spoken by Montague will also help you:

Many a morning hath he there been seen,
With tears augmenting the fresh morning's dew,
Adding to clouds more clouds with his deep sighs.
Away from light steals home my heavy son
And private in his chamber pens himself,
Shuts up his windows, locks fair daylight out
And makes him an artificial night.

Have you worked out how some people behave when they think they are in love?
Remember this, because Romeo will change when he really falls in love with Juliet.

Activities for Act 1

Writing a missing scene

Not everything that happens in a play is shown on stage. The play would be very long.
Imagine an Elizabethan groundling having to stand for longer than THREE hours!
On page 7 Paris asks Capulet if he has thought about him marrying Juliet. Capulet invites him to the party, telling him to try to **impress** Juliet.
On pages 9 and 10 Lady Capulet tells Juliet that she must take a look at Paris to see if she can love him and marry him. *What's missing?* The scene where Capulet tells his wife about Paris and what she must do.

Draw the scene in the comic strip below. They might talk about:

- what she should say to Juliet
- what Paris is like
- Juliet's age

Activities for Act I

Invitations and masks

Look at pages 7 and 8.
Here we learn that Capulet is going to have 'an old accustom'd feast', in other words – a party!
He sends his Servant off with the list of guests.

1 Imagine that Capulet sent invitations, instead of a list. You're going to design the invitation that he might send to his friends.
What would you expect to find on an invitation? Think about the answers to these questions. They might help.

- How would the guest know who had sent the invitation?
- How would the guest know where the party was to take place?
- How would he know the exact day and date of the party?
- How would the guest know what time the party was to begin and end?
- How would he know what to wear?
- How would he know whether there was food or drink at the party?

Remember to think about the information on the invitation, but also think about the design. You might want to have it in a special shape or in a particular colour. You might also want to talk over your ideas with a partner before you begin.

When you have finished that, look at page 11. Have you noticed that the party-goers are wearing masks? This was to disguise themselves and to have fun!

2 Design the masks for Romeo and Juliet. Or if you prefer, you can choose others, like Tybalt, for example. Try to make the mask bring out the character who wears it. Remember to think about shape and colour when you plan them out.
Ask the Art/Technology teacher to help you with materials for your masks. You might put them on display and talk about your ideas as a whole class.

Activities for Act 1

In the meantime

Shakespeare meant his play to be acted on stage. We are reading it, but now it's time to think about **staging a scene**.

Look at page 12 again. This is where Romeo first sees Juliet. He asks a Servingman who the lady is '**that doth enrich the hand of yonder knight.**'
He talks about her beauty and falls in love!
But Tybalt and Capulet begin talking. Capulet has to stop Tybalt from fighting with Romeo.
Have you noticed that the next time we see Romeo, he has managed to get close to Juliet, and he is talking to her! The dance where she was with the knight must have finished.

What you have to do now is show the party scene, making sure that each character is doing something while the others speak!

1 In groups of six, sort out your parts: Romeo, Servingman, Knight, Tybalt, Capulet and Juliet.

- Romeo and the Servingman are talking – in the meantime, Juliet and the Knight are dancing; what are Tybalt and Capulet doing?
- Later on, Tybalt and Capulet are talking – in the meantime Romeo manages to get near to Juliet; how?
- Romeo now talks to Juliet – in the meantime, what is Tybalt doing!
- The characters who don't speak will be **miming** their parts – that is they will be using hand movements and facial expressions, but will also be pretending to talk, making no noise!

2 Once you have practised, show the scene to the rest of the class. Be prepared to explain why you chose certain movements and positions.

3 Watch other groups as well. This way, you learn from others and improve your work.

Activities for Act 1

Love at first sight!

Look again at the party scene on page 12.
Here Romeo sees Juliet for the first time. He falls in love with her as soon as he sees her face.

1 Try to describe Juliet by reading Romeo's words and putting them into your own.

Answer the questions below. They will help you.

- How do we know that she makes everything brighter and more cheerful?
- How do we know that she is something special?
- Why does a dove seem more beautiful than a crow? Think of colours.

Think about the **symbols**: torches, a rich jewel, a snowy dove, crows.
These will also help you write up the description.

2 Now that you have done that, read Capulet's description of Romeo and put that into your own words.

Capulet is very *sly*. Read what he says to Tybalt on pages 12 and 13. Find lines that tell you he would be happy if Tybalt fought Romeo somewhere else!

Activities for Act 2

Sunday ... Monday ...

They were very busy days for Romeo and Juliet.
Fill in the blanks to help you remind yourself of what happened. The words below will help you.

Romeo was in love with _____ . Benvolio persuaded him to go to a party. There Romeo fell in love with _____ . She had been told by her _____ to look at a young, handsome man called _____ , because she might have to marry him. BUT ... at her party, she fell in love with _____ . They made plans for their _____ . They left each other early Monday _____ .

Juliet   wedding   Rosaline   mother   Paris
morning   Romeo

Now write Romeo's diary entry for Sunday ... Monday. Use the words above to help you.

Activities for Act 2

Do you think I am doing the right thing?

Read pages 12–17 again.

1 Write the letter that Juliet might send to a **problem page** about what happened. Remember – Juliet is only 13.

To help you, think of:

- what you thought when Romeo 'chatted you up'
- what you felt when you found out his name was *Montague*
- what he said to you under the balcony
- what you said to him
- what your worries were and still are.

2 Then write the answer from an **agony aunt**.

Use the words below to help you.

Dear Agony Aunt,
Something wonderful happened last night! I was at a party my father planned when......

Dear Juliet,
You are very young to get married but......

Activities for Act 2

Sticks and stones may break my bones, but names will never hurt me!

Have you heard that said? With a partner, decide what that means. Better still, decide whether it's true!

Names are important. If someone insults you, then you are hurt or angry.
But even people's first and last names are important.

1 At home, ask your parents why they chose your name and then report back to the class – it might be that they liked it or that they named you after someone. What else did your parents say?

2 Can you come up with names that you think are old fashioned?

3 What names are really popular at the moment?
In groups, decide why these names are popular. Is it because there are famous people with the name?

4 Keep in your groups, but this time make sure that someone writes down the ideas to report back to the rest of the class. Remember as well, that your answers must not insult or offend anyone in the room!
Think about:

- When can you call someone by their first name?
- Would you call your teacher by her/his first name? Why not?
- Would you call a person you have only just met by her/his first name?
- What names make you laugh? Why is that?
- What nicknames do you have for people?
- Do you have any other ideas about names?

Activities for Act 2

What's in a name?

1 On page 15, read Juliet's words, from '**O Romeo . . .** to **smell as sweet.**'
Put these into your own words. Do you agree with her?

2 Now read Romeo's words, from '**I take thee . . .** to **Romeo.**'
Put these into your own words. How is Romeo feeling?

The trouble is that names are very important in Verona.

3 In the two columns below, write the names that each family hates. It doesn't just have to be people's names, it can be words. Remember Tybalt said he hated the word PEACE!

Capulet	Montague

Now you'll know the answer to: **What's in a name?**

Activities for Act 2

I challenge you ...

Do you remember what Tybalt wanted to do when he heard Romeo's voice at the party?
On page 20, Benvolio says that Tybalt has sent a letter to Romeo, challenging him to fight.
Imagine that you are Tybalt.
Write the challenge that you will send Romeo.
Remember you will have to write:

- Will you draw anything on your letter to scare Romeo?
- What colour paper might you use?
- Will you sign off with an insult?
- Will you show off and brag about winning?

You might make a display of all the letters, so that the class can talk about them.

Activities for Act 2

Crack the code!

Romeo and Juliet have to keep their plans a secret.

We know that Romeo has told the Nurse the plans for the wedding, but just imagine that he gave the Nurse a letter as well.

- He wouldn't write it so that she could read it would he?
- He would write it so that only Juliet could read it.

Here's the letter, but it's in code.

Work out the code and write the letter in English. The letters of the alphabet are here to help you.

A B C D E F G H I J K L M N O P Q R S T U V W X Y Z

23 22 26 9/17 6 15 18 22 7/, 14 2/15 12 5 22,

18/19 26 5 22/7 26 15 16 22 23/7 12/ 2 12 6 9/
13 6 9 8 22./ 18/ 7 12 15 23/ 19 22 9/ 7 19 26 7/
2 12 6/ 14 6 8 7 / 14 22 22 7 / 14 22 26 7/ 21 9 18 26 9/
15 26 6 9 22 13 24 22' 8 / 24 22 15 15/ 7 19 18 8/
26 21 7 22 9 13 12 12 13./ 7 19 22 9 22/ 4 22/4 18 15 15/
25 22/ 14 26 9 9 18 22 23/.
2 12 6 9/ 13 6 9 8 22/ 4 18 15 15/ 21 22 7 24 19 /26/
15 26 23 23 22 9/ 4 19 18 24 19/ 18/ 4 18 15 15/
6 8 22/ 7 12/ 24 15 18 14 25/ 18 13 7 12/ 2 12 6 9/
25 22 23 9 12 12 14/ 15 26 7 22 9/ 7 12 13 18 20 19 7/.

9 12 14 22 12

Activities for Act 2

A friend in need ... is a friend indeed

Romeo is in need of help. He turns to Friar Laurence, because he trusts him.

Using pages 18 and 19, find the lines that prove these sentences correct:

1. The Friar gets up early.
2. He knows a lot about plants – which ones can cure and which ones can kill.
3. He knows about Romeo's love for Rosaline.
4. He is pleased that Romeo has given up on Rosaline.
5. He likes things said plainly.
6. He is shocked at Romeo's change of heart – first Rosaline, now Juliet.
7. He is happy to help if it will end the trouble between the two families – the Montagues and the Capulets.
8. He prefers to take his time over things.

Would you trust him? Is he sensible? Do you think he is a good friend to Romeo and Juliet?

Activities for Act 2

The first sign of madness

What's the first sign of madness?
Talking to yourself!
What's the second?
Answering!

That's an old joke! Lots of people talk to themselves. Sometimes it's thoughts in your head. Sometimes it's thoughts spoken out loud, when no-one else can hear!

1 Think of times when you have 'talked' to yourself. What did you come up with – times when you were travelling and day-dreamed; times when you were cross with someone and you were going over what you would say to that person?
Share your ideas with the class.

2 When have you seen other people talking to themselves? When they are walking around shops; driving a car; busy doing something difficult?
With a partner, think of the reasons why we all do it?

When someone talks to themselves on stage it is sometimes called a **monologue**. Now look again at pages 18 and 19. You have already decided what you think of the Friar. Now imagine that you are him. You have just been told by Romeo that he wants to marry Juliet and he needs your help!

3 Write the **monologue** that you, as Friar Laurence, will say to yourself while you think this news through. Put in all the information from pages 18 and 19, so that it is clear what you know. Imagine what the Friar feels now that he has agreed to help.
You could read your monologue out in front of the class.

Activities for Act 2

In a minute, in a minute!

With a partner, talk about times when you might have heard someone say the words 'in a minute'.
Was it when someone tried to rush somebody?

On pages 24 and 25, the Nurse makes Juliet wait longer than a minute!
Make a list of nine ways in which the Nurse teases Juliet and makes her wait for the wedding plans.
These lines will help you:

- Do you not see that I am out of breath?
- You know not how to choose a man
- Have you dined at home?
- How my head aches
- My back o'th'other side; O! my back!
- Like an honest gentleman, and a courteous, and a kind, and a handsome ...
- Where is your mother?
- Are you so hot?
- Henceforward do your messages yourself.

In pairs, act out the scene using Modern English.

Activities for Act 2

Party dresses/wedding dresses

Designing a costume for an actress to wear on stage is very important indeed.
The dresses that Juliet wears at her party and at her wedding tell us a lot about her and why Romeo fell in love with her.
The designer thinks about the shape of the dress, its colour, its length.
She/he will think about Juliet's hair, her jewellery, her shoes, even whether she should carry anything!
Juliet's age is also important – she isn't 14 yet!
Now you're going to design the two dresses.

The party dress

This dress is what Juliet is wearing when Romeo first sees her and falls in love so quickly! It must be very beautiful. You could draw the dress and then colour it in. You MUST be able to explain to a partner WHY you chose to design it in a special way.
You might also include details like, hair, jewellery, fans, bags.

The wedding dress

This dress is the one that Juliet wears to Friar Laurence's cell to marry Romeo.
Will it be as beautiful as the party dress?
Remember that no-one at home, except the Nurse, knows what she is going to do.
They think that she is going to visit Friar Laurence, who is a holy man!
Think carefully now about what the dress will look like.
Think about what she might carry on a visit to a holy man.
Again, when you have drawn it, you must be able to explain why you chose the design, the colours, and any things that she might be carrying.
You might also talk about her hairstyle.

Activities for Act 3

It had to happen – the turning point!

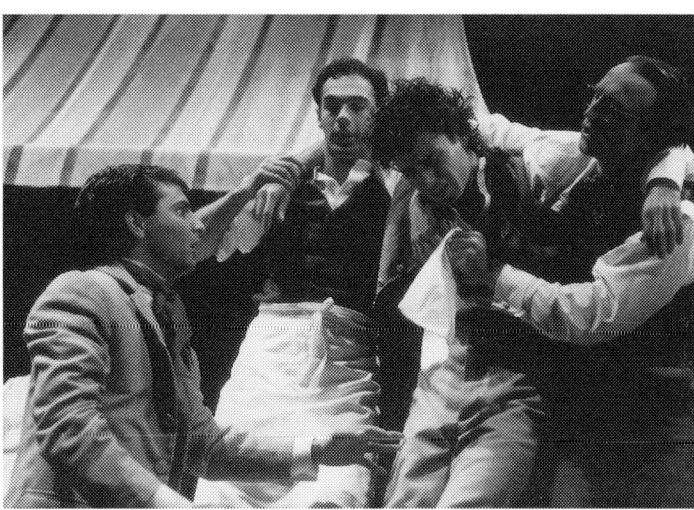

If the Chorus hadn't already told us the story, we might have thought that this play was a comedy! After all, there could have been a happy ending – that is up until Act 3: Scene 1.

In groups, using pages 27 to 30, find **proof** that the deaths of Mercutio and Tybalt *had* to happen. Present your **evidence** to the class.

The answers to these questions will help:

1 What was the weather like? Why would this make the youths ready for trouble?
2 Why has Tybalt come to fight with Romeo?
3 How does Mercutio irritate Tybalt?
4 Why does Mercutio fight instead of Romeo?
5 Why does Romeo try to stop the fight?

Find **evidence** that Benvolio and Romeo tried to stop the trouble.
Finally, why did Romeo end up fighting and killing Tybalt?

Activities for Act 3

Television brings you up-to-date news

Television news bulletins are an important way of learning about the news.
Sometimes, people prefer to **listen** to the news than to buy a newspaper and **read** the news.

1 Why do you think that is? With a partner make a list of about FOUR reasons that you can share with the class.

2 Imagine that you are Verona's television news reporter. You job is to tell the story of what happened when Tybalt murdered Mercutio, then afterwards, how Romeo murdered Tybalt.
Your boss has told you that you have three minutes to stand in front of the camera and report the story.

- Read the scenes again and try to get as much information as possible.
- Write down what you might say and then read it over until you can say it without looking at your notes.
- You might want to ask another pupil to act the part of an eye witness (that is someone who was actually there at the time and saw exactly what happened). You can then interview that person.
- Try timing your report. Is it about three minutes?

3 When you're ready, present your bulletin to the rest of the class.
If you have a video camera, you might film the report.
What did the class think of your work?

Remember that when you listen to their opinions, you are **evaluating** your work.
You are thinking about what your class is saying and you are using their ideas to make your own work better.

Activities for Act 3

Banished ...

'Immediately, we do exile him hence: else when he's found, that hour is his last.'

These are the Prince's words when he finds out that Romeo has killed Tybalt.
Read page 31 again.

- Why doesn't the Prince want to execute Romeo?
- Did you notice that Benvolio doesn't tell the whole truth?
- Can you see what he misses out?

He doesn't say that Mercutio tried to get Tybalt to fight with him!
Did you notice that Lady Capulet wants Romeo dead, because she doesn't trust Benvolio's account?

The people of Verona will know the Prince's decision. To make sure that they listen to the Prince and obey him, what might he have put up in the streets?

Posters

Design the poster that could go up in the streets.

1 This poster must describe Romeo. It must give information about his crime, and tell people what his punishment is.

2 You will need to tell the people of Verona what to do if they spot Romeo in their town.

3 Remember to think about the print size; the position of the printed words; any signature; any drawings.

4 You might plan it out first and then draw the final piece on large paper.
Your teacher might make a display of all the posters for the whole class to look at.

Activities for Act 3

There are two sides to every story

Now that Romeo is banished to Mantua, the two families – the Capulets and the Montagues – will have a lot to talk about.

The Montagues, Romeo's family – how will they be feeling? Jot down a few ideas.

The Capulets, Tybalt's family – how will they be feeling? Jot down a few ideas.

In groups of FOUR, decide who will take the parts of Montague, Lady Montague, Capulet, Lady Capulet.

1 Go over the ideas you have written down. Try to develop these into two scripts, showing the **two sides to the story** of Tybalt's murder and Romeo's exile.
Remember that drama scripts are set out like this:

In the Montague house:

Lady Montague: Oh my son, my son. How will we live without him?
Montague: Listen, love, maybe we should think we're lucky …

When you have finished that one, the next will be:

In the Capulet house:

Lady Capulet: I don't believe it. He should have been executed!
Capulet: I know, but …

2 Once you have written the two scripts, practise them, then act them out in front of your class. Did you make it clear that there were **two sides to the story**?

Activities for Act 3

What is she trying to say?

This must be what Juliet is thinking when the Nurse comes home after fetching the rope ladder.

1 Read pages 32 and 33 again. What you must find out is how many mistakes Juliet makes when she is listening to the Nurse.
These lines might help you:

- he's dead (Who does Juliet think is dead? Who is really dead?)
- he's gone, he's killed, he's dead! (Again, who does Juliet think has gone? Who has really been killed?)
- O Romeo ... who ever would have thought it? (Thought what? What does Juliet think here; what does the Nurse mean?)
- Hath Romeo slain himself? (What does Juliet think has happened?)
- I saw the wound (What wound does the Nurse mean? What wound does Juliet think she means?)
- a bloody piteous corse (Whose corpse does the Nurse mean? Whose does Juliet think of?)
- O Tybalt! (Now what does Juliet think?)

Finally, Juliet finds out that 'Tybalt is gone, and Romeo is banished'. She also learns that Romeo killed Tybalt.

2 Try to work out how Juliet feels now that her cousin is killed and her husband is banished.
To help you, read the words beginning: O serpent heart ...

3 Can you write down all the opposites she uses? What is she trying to say about Romeo here?

4 Can you find the words that the Nurse uses that make Juliet change her mind about Romeo?

5 If you were Juliet now, what would you do?

Activities for Act 3

I don't believe this has happened

This must be what Juliet is thinking now that she knows Tybalt has been murdered by her husband Romeo, and he is to be banished from Verona.

Imagine you are Juliet. You are speaking your thoughts aloud on stage – this is called a **soliloquy**.
Read pages 32, 33 and 34 to help you write the thoughts before you speak them to the class.
You might write about:

- how much you were looking forward to seeing Romeo again – remember the Nurse went off to fetch the rope ladder to let Romeo climb into your bedroom
- how confused you were when the Nurse first came back
- how upset you were when you realised the truth
- how mad you were at the Nurse when she insulted Romeo
- how you feel now that the Nurse has said she will find Romeo to comfort you.

Now you're ready to act Juliet's thoughts out.

Activities for Act 3

Writing a letter of despair

That will be the type of letter that Romeo will write, as he is hiding in Friar Laurence's cell.
You have put yourself into Juliet's thoughts and character; now put yourself into Romeo's mind!

1 Write this letter to Juliet, explaining what has happened and how you feel.

Think about a few things to help you do this:

- how did you come to kill Tybalt? You will want to explain that to Juliet.
- how did you manage to run to the Friar's cell without anyone seeing you?
- how do you feel, now that you know you have to go to Mantua, never to return to Verona?
- are you worried about what Juliet is thinking about you – after all, you have murdered her cousin.
- will you tell her how much you love her?
- will you try to make any plans for the future?

2 **Draft** your letter first and discuss it with a partner. Listen to your partner's opinions of your letter, then when you redraft it, add any details that you missed out the first time.

Remember when you write your letter, take care with your spelling and punctuation.

3 Now read your letter to the rest of the class.

Activities for Act 3

You've got a lot to be thankful for!

People often say this. When would you say you have heard these words?
Did you think of times when you are complaining about things? Perhaps you have been told that you should be thankful for what you've got.
That is really what the Friar is telling Romeo.

1 Read pages 36 and 37 and look at how Romeo is acting. Make a list of the things he is doing.
These will help you:

- There on the ground, with his own tears made drunk.
- Blubbering and weeping ...
- [*Romeo draws his sword*]
- thy wild acts denote the unreasonable fury of a beast.

2 Now that you have done that, turn to the Friar's words, where he tells Romeo he should be grateful that he is not to be executed.
What arguments does he put to Romeo?
Make a list of them. These will help you:

- wilt thou slay thyself? And slay thy lady that in thy life lives, By doing damned hate upon thyself?
- thy Juliet is alive,
- Tybalt would kill thee, But thou slew'st Tybalt;
- The law that threatened death becomes thy friend

3 What would you think if you were Romeo now?
Would you feel better knowing you were going to see Juliet?
Would you have hope for the future?
Talk about your ideas with your partner or with the class.

Activities for Act 3

What's the plan? – another missing scene

We know that Friar Laurence has told Romeo that he must go to Juliet, but that he must not stay too long. He must go before the sun rises.
We know that Friar Laurence will send Romeo's servant to Mantua every now and then, to give Romeo news.
We know that he is going to try to arrange for Romeo to return and tell everyone that Juliet is his wife.
We know that the Nurse has to go and tell Juliet what the plan is going to be.

1 In pairs, write the scene between the Nurse and Juliet, when the Nurse returns from Friar Laurence's cell to tell Juliet the plan.

- Remember that Juliet will want to know how Romeo is.
- Remember that she will be upset at first.
- How will she feel when she finds out that Romeo is coming to see her after all?
- How will she feel when she knows he has to leave before dawn?
- Will she have any hope for the future?
- Try to show all her feelings in the script.

2 Once you have done that, practise reading it together and when you are ready, act or read it out in front of the class. What did they think of it?

Are you pleased with what you have done?
If you are, well done!
If not, what will you do next time to improve your work?

Activities for Act 3

Parting is such sweet sorrow!

Juliet said that when she was on her balcony talking to Romeo. That was Sunday evening, after the party.
They got married on Monday.
Romeo killed Tybalt on Monday!
And now it's only Tuesday, and they have to leave each other again – but this time they don't know how long for.

1 In the bubbles below, write down their thoughts, now they have to part.

Remember:

- Juliet pretended it was still night
- Romeo agreed and said that he'd risk death and stay with Juliet
- Juliet changed her mind and said he must go.

2 Is this the saddest scene so far? Talk about this in class.

Activities for Act 3

The story so far

The paragraph below tells the story up until page 40.

There are ten words missing. Choose the most suitable words from the lists below. (Choose from list **A** to fill the space at **A**, and so on.)

> There is trouble on the streets of Verona. The Montagues and the Capulets fight. When the Prince comes, he tells Montague and Capulet that they will **A** if trouble breaks out again. We meet Romeo who thinks he's in love with **B**. Benvolio persuades him to go to a **C** at the Capulet's house to see other girls. There Romeo meets Juliet and falls in love. He finds out that she is the daughter of his **D**. He goes into the **E** where he sees Juliet on her **F**. They talk and decide to **G**. With the help of Juliet's **H** and Friar Laurence, the two young lovers do get married.
> But ... in a fight, Romeo kills Tybalt, a Capulet, and he is **I**. Before leaving for Mantua, he spends one **J** with Juliet. They are both desperate to be together in the future.

A	B	C	D	E
pay a fine	Rose	picnic	best friend	garden
be put to death	Rosaline	party	enemy	courtyard
be sent away	Rosalind	magic show	cousin	dining room

F	G	H	I	J
balcony	run away	nurse	wounded	weekend
horse	marry	father	banished	hour
window sill	go on holiday	mother	captured	night

33

© HODDER & STOUGHTON LTD 1999.
Copying permitted in purchasing school only.

Activities for Act 3

Parents!

Everybody has arguments at some time with their parents. Can you remember a time when you didn't like what your parents told you to do?

1 Why do parents and children argue at times? In groups, **brainstorm** some ideas.
Someone in the group write the ideas down to report back to the class.
(When you **brainstorm**, you put all your ideas together in no particular order!)
What did you come up with?

Now think about Juliet in Act 3: Scene 5.
Her parents have told her she has to marry Paris – trouble is, she's already married to Romeo!

2 In groups of FOUR, act out this scene, using modern English.
Read it through first and work out what you want to say. Remember you don't have to say everything. You just need to put the idea of the scene across.

3 You might now want to **improvise**. This means that you will say some things without really having prepared them, just to test out what they sound like!
Work on this, deciding how you want the characters to come across.
Think about:

- Juliet: will she be angry? forceful? determined? quiet? mad with everyone?
- Capulet: will he be proud? angry? violent?
- Lady Capulet: will she be cross? pleasant to Juliet?
- Nurse: will she be protecting Juliet? quiet?

Decide how you will act it out, how your characters will move around. When you are satisfied, you can show your work to the rest of the class.

Activities for Act 3

Continue the scene . . .

You have used the text to act out Act 3: Scene 5. Now in the same groups, take the scene further on.

1 Script the conversation between Lady Capulet and Capulet after they have both stormed out of the room. They will be very angry with Juliet for disobeying them.
They will talk over what she said and how they are going to deal with it.
(The two of you who are playing Juliet and the Nurse can listen and offer ideas and advice.)

2 Once you have done that . . . the Nurse must come in. What will she tell them?

Read the lines on page 43 again, where Juliet says:

Go in; and tell my lady I am gone,
Having displeas'd my father, to Laurence' cell,
To make confession and to be absolv'd.

Now you know what the Nurse will say!

3 While the Nurse is talking to Lady Capulet and Capulet, what will Juliet be doing? She should continue acting in the background.

4 Run through your piece a few times, until you are sure it is ready to be shown.

5 Then present it to the class.
What did they think of it?
What did you think of the other groups' ideas?

Activities for Act 4

A desperate plan!

Here is the plan that Friar Laurence comes up with.
Some of the words have their letters jumbled up.
Sort them out, so that you understand what Juliet must do!
To do this, use the words that the Friar speaks on page 45, Act 4: Scene 1.

> The Friar tells Juliet that she must go home, and agree to marry **rsiPa** on Thursday. On Wednesday **ihgtn**, she must make sure that she is **oenla** in her room. There she must take out the bottle of **qouilr** and drink it. Once the liquid goes through her veins, she will have no **uselp**, no **thmraw**, no **bearht**. She will look like she is **aedd**. The liquid will work for forty two **rshou**. She will wake up in the Capulet **ualvt**. Meanwhile the Friar will send **ttreesl** to Romeo to tell him about the plan. He will also tell Romeo to come to Verona and they will both watch until Juliet wakes up. Romeo will then take Juliet to **Mtauan**.

Now you are sure of the plan!

Think about Juliet at this point in the play.
She knows the plan. She will be worried. She has no choice.
Try to draw the **images** that might be going through her mind right now. **Images** are pictures that she will be thinking of – scary ones, happy ones!

With a partner, talk about the images.
Be prepared to explain why you picked certain images.

Activities for Act 4

Sending a telegram

Imagine that the Friar could send a telegram instead of a letter to Romeo in Mantua.
A telegram is much shorter than a letter and gives only the necessary facts. You have to pay for every word!
Read the letter below, then make it into a telegram.

> Dear Romeo,
>
> Juliet has been to visit me in my cell. She has told me that she must marry Paris. You remember Paris? He is a fine young fellow, but even so, he cannot marry Juliet. So, I have come up with a plan – Juliet is going to drink a liquid tomorrow night, when she is in her room alone. This liquid will make her fall asleep and seem like she is dead. It will only last 42 hours but it will stop her from marrying Paris. She will be placed in the Capulet vault, because everyone will think that she is dead. We have to be there when she wakes up, so that you can take her with you to Mantua. Come here to my cell late at night. Make sure no-one sees you. We will go to the vault and wait until she wakes, then you can be together, until I manage to persuade your two families and the Prince to let you back into Verona.
> Until then
> Friar Laurence.

Charge 10p for every word used. Add up the cost.
Who, in your class, has sent the cheapest telegram? Does it give all the information needed?

Activities for Act 4

What are they thinking now?

At this point in the play, at the end of Act 4: Scenes 1, 2 and 3, stop and think about the different characters.
They all have opinions and ideas about what is happening. They don't know what others are thinking. We can work that out, because the audience knows far more than the characters on stage.

1 Below, some thoughts are written down.
You must try to work out whose thoughts they are. Which ones belong to which characters?
To help read pages 44–46 again.
The characters are: Lady Capulet, Capulet, Juliet, Paris, the Nurse and Friar Laurence.

a I am so happy. I am going to get married to the lady of my dreams, and earlier than I expected. This is such good news.

b I'm not sure that I can go through with this. I don't really think that I have a choice, but I am so worried.

c Thank goodness that girl came to see sense. I was really cross with her. Still, she is fine now and everything will turn out well. I'm looking forward to the wedding!

d Why does he want to bring the wedding forward? I tried to get him to leave it as it was. Anyway, I suppose it will turn out for the best, Juliet seems to have accepted her father's wishes.

e I hope this goes well. I know my plants and potions, but this is something special. I hope Romeo can get here on time!

f Well, I did tell her she should marry Paris, now that Romeo isn't around. I just hope that this works out for her. She is so young!

2 That is what the characters might be thinking.
What are you thinking at this point?
Do you think that Juliet has a choice? What else could she do if she didn't want to drink the liquid? Write down some ideas and share them with the class.

Activities for Act 4

Good news!

At least Paris thinks it is.
Capulet has just said: 'I will to Paris to prepare him against tomorrow.'
The wedding will now be earlier than Paris expected.
Paris thought he was going to marry Juliet on Thursday; now he is going to marry her on Wednesday.
Why does Capulet want to marry Juliet off so quickly? What is he worried about?

1 In pairs, decide on your parts: Capulet and Paris.
Improvise the scene that might take place at Paris' house, when Capulet arrives to tell Paris he can wed Juliet earlier.

2 Remember when you **improvise**, you try out some ideas together without having planned too much. If you are pleased with the ideas, work on them, perhaps change them or maybe add some.

- Think about the way that Capulet will speak to Paris.
  What reasons will he give Paris for changing the arrangements?
  What will he tell Paris to do tomorrow morning?

- What will Paris say to Capulet when he finds out?
  Will he be pleased?
  Might he be puzzled?
  Will he ask about Juliet, how she is perhaps?
  Will he be polite and ask about Lady Capulet, especially how she is after the shock of Tybalt's death?

3 Try your ideas out.

4 When you are ready, show your piece to the class.
What did they think of it?

Activities for Act 4

Juliet's worries

Read page 47, Act 4: Scene 3 again.

1 Write down what Juliet is worried about. You will have to look closely at the lines, but here are some to help you:

- What if this mixture do not work at all?
- What if it be poison ...
- Lest in this marriage he should be dishonour'd
- How if ... I wake before the time that Romeo come?
- Shall I not then be stifled ...
  And die there strangled?
- Is it not like that I ... run mad?
- Shall I not be distraught?
- And madly play with my forefathers' joints?
- And pluck the mangled Tybalt from his shroud?

This is the stuff that horror films are made of!

2 Look again at the scene. What does she do, in case the poison doesn't work?
How would you describe Juliet now?

Activities for Act 4

Thought tracking

When Juliet is found 'dead', what characters are on stage? Read page 48 again to find out.

You will have noticed that the Nurse, Lady Capulet, Capulet, Paris and the Friar are on stage.

1 You will need to work in groups of five, each one taking a character. There is no need to have Juliet – imagine that the body is in a certain place.

2 Now form a **freeze frame** around the 'corpse'.

> Remember that a **freeze frame** is like a photograph – it shows the characters, but they are not moving. The freeze frame should try to show how each character is feeling. This can be done by thinking about the way you stand, what you do with your arms and how your face looks.

3 Hold your freeze frame for about five seconds.

4 After that, each character must speak ONE sentence that shows what that character is thinking now that Juliet is 'dead'. Each character speaks alone.

5 The group must then decide how to go off stage – or return to seats in the classroom.

Remember that this is a sad scene and every movement you make is important to make the mood right.

Activities for Act 5

A letter explaining everything

Look at page 49, Act 5: Scene 1.
Romeo has just heard that Juliet is dead. He loves his parents so he knows that anything he does, he must explain to them. That's why he asks for 'ink and paper'.

He must write to his parents telling them what has happened. Imagine that you are Romeo and you have to write this letter that tells your parents what you have been doing and what you plan to do. It will be hard to choose the right words, but you know your parents deserve an explanation.

Plan your letter carefully. Think about:

- how you will tell them that you got married to Juliet
- how you will explain why you killed Tybalt
- how you will tell them about the Friar's part in all of your plans
- how you will tell them that you are going to Verona to kill yourself and lie by Juliet's side in the vault
- what you will ask them to do now that you know you will die with Juliet.

Draft it out first, until you are pleased with it.
Share your work with a partner, looking at your choice of words. Was it hard to find just the right words?

Activities for Act 5

Just a note to say that . . .

Look at page 50 again. Here we see Friar Laurence being told by Friar John that he couldn't take the letter to Romeo in Mantua.
Friar Laurence is very unhappy. He knows that Juliet will wake up in three hours.

This time he says he will send another letter, but he won't have time to write a long one, will he? He will be busy working out how to get Juliet out of the monument and back to his cell!

Write his message on a postcard.
This time, plans will change:

Answer these questions to help you.

1 Will he tell Romeo he has written before?
2 Will he go into detail about Juliet's death potion?
3 Where will Romeo have to meet Juliet now?
4 Will he still have to come in darkness?

43

ACTIVITIES for Act 5

What Balthasar saw

Look again at page 51 – where Romeo and Balthasar arrive at the vault.
Read it again.

Balthasar is told to leave.

- What does he have to take to Romeo's father?
- Does he go straight away?
- From his hiding place, he sees everything that happens, up until Romeo carries Paris into the tomb (on page 52).

Imagine that you are Balthasar.
You are asked to give an **eyewitness account** of what you saw at the tomb.
This means that you will have to say exactly what you *saw*.
You can also add *how you felt* when you saw the two youths fighting, and Paris killed.

1 For your work, you will have to read the scene a few times to make sense of what Balthasar saw.
Make notes on the first and second reading.

2 After that, write it up as if you are speaking it out to someone.

3 Read it through, to make sure that it makes sense and that you haven't missed any details.

Activities for Act 5

Stop right there! Don't do it!

How to break all the rules!

Nobody, in our time, would even think about standing up in a Shakespeare play and shouting at the actors! Think what would happen if you did that.
Everyone would look at you!
You would probably get thrown out of the theatre!
The actors might carry on, but they would wonder what was happening!
I bet that there have been times when lots of people have wanted to say something, though. It's only the **rules of behaviour** in a theatre that stop us from shouting out.

1 What are the **rules of behaviour** in a theatre?
Discuss this with a partner, thinking about for example, talking during a performance, eating, rustling packets, getting up to go out, moving around in your seat. Report to the rest of the class.

2 Look at page 52.
Imagine that you have been listening to Romeo. Imagine that you reach the line:

Arms, take your last embrace!

You can't take any more!
You stand up and yell: **No! Stop Romeo! Don't do it!**
Everyone freezes, but you carry on ...
What will you say?
You'll have to tell him that Juliet is alive now. You'll have to tell him what's been going on!
Write down the words you would say.

3 When you think you can say them out loud in front of the class, present your showstopper!

What did they think of it?
Just remember – don't try this in the real thing!

Activities for Act 5

The story is over . . .

The passage below tells the rest of the story. There are TEN words missing. Choose the most suitable from the lists below. (Choose from list **A** to fill space **A** and so on.)

Romeo has left for **A**. Capulet has agreed that Paris can **B** Juliet. She refuses and goes to **C** for help. He tells her to go home, agree to the **D** and drink a liquid that will make her sleep for **E**. He will send a **F** to Romeo to tell him that he must come to the Capulet **G**, so that when Juliet wakes, they will be there. BUT ... the letter never reaches Romeo. Balthasar tells Romeo that Juliet has **H**. Romeo buys some poison from a **I**, travels to the Capulet's vault and kills Paris. He swallows the poison and dies. Juliet wakes up and kills herself with a **J**. Their deaths make the Montagues and Capulets realise how silly they have been. They make up and agree never to cause trouble again.

A	B	C	D	E
Verona	talk to	her father	plan	a week
Mantua	meet	Rosaline	wedding	a hundred years
his house	marry	Friar Laurence	holiday	forty-two hours
the Prince's palace	date	the Nurse	visit	a day

F	G	H	I	J
letter	garden	died	chemist	gun
person	house	left Verona	grocer	dagger
card	vault	run away	shop	bottle of poison
telegram	party	got married	Friar	kiss

After the play activities

Stop! Cut the action!

Have you ever heard that said?
Directors of films or television programmes might say those words.
What do you think they want to do at this point?

- **a** Go for dinner?
- **b** Sack all the actors?
- **c** Stop the filming and try it again?
- **d** Act out the scene, changing a few things?
- **e** Cut the film inside the cameras?

Hopefully you answered **c** and **d**.

Just imagine that a director changed her mind during the filming of *Romeo and Juliet*.
Just imagine that she decided the ending was too sad.

You are the story writer. She tells you that you must write the play, making the ending happy!

1 In a story form, write the happy ending. You will have to change the story from the **turning point** in the play – that is where Tybalt murders Mercutio and Romeo murders Tybalt.

A **turning point** is the point in the play where the story changes mood – with the murder of Mercutio, the play becomes a **tragedy** (a sad story); before that it could have been a **comedy** (a story with a happy ending).

2 After you have written your story, swap it with a partner. See if you came up with similar ideas.
Try to decide what parts you liked best in each other's stories.

3 Report what you have done to the rest of the class. See if they came up with similar ideas.

After the play activities

Here lies the body of . . . 1

In every graveyard, you will find **gravestones** or **tombstones**.

There are words written on these to tell us who is buried underneath.
These words usually give us the following information:

- the name of the person
- the date she/he was born
- the date she/he died
- the name of her/his mother and father; wife/husband.

Sometimes there is a poem or a few extra words about that person. These are called an **epitaph**.

Here is the **epitaph** that might have appeared on Tybalt's gravestone. Some of the details are made up. . . .

Here lies the body of

Tybalt Capulet

Beloved nephew of
The Lord and Lady Capulet.
Cousin of Juliet Capulet.

Born in 1476
Died in 1494

Cut down in his youth
by an enemy's hand.

May he sleep in peace.

(Continued on Sheet 2)

After the play activities

Here lies the body of ... 2

(Continued from Sheet 1)

Try to fill in the blank spaces on Mercutio's epitaph.
The words at the end are there to help you.

Here lies the _____ of

Mercutio Escalus

Beloved _____ of
Prince Escalus of Verona,
and friend of Romeo _____

Born in 1477
Died in 1494

Cruelly _____ by an enemy

May he _____ in peace

| kinsman | Montague | murdered | rest | body |

Now try to make up the **epitaphs** that might appear on the gravestones of Romeo and Juliet.

After the play activities

Read all about it!

Reading newspapers is an important way of finding out what is going on in our country and in the world.

1 Look at the front page of a newspaper. Make a list of about FIVE things you can see.

2 When you have done this, show your list to another pupil. Have you written down the same things?

You might have noticed:

- the name of the paper
- the date and the price
- headlines
- pictures
- writing in columns
- different kinds of **fonts** (that is the print used).

3 Now, try to make the front page of a newspaper that might appear after the death of Romeo and Juliet.
It might help to ask yourself the following questions:

- What might the paper be called, if they lived in Verona?
- What date would the paper have, if the play took place sometime in July?
- What might the headline be, if it has to make people want to read about the death of the two young lovers?
- Would the Nurse sell her story to the paper?
- Would Friar Laurence sell his story to the paper?
- Would the paper write anything about Capulet and Montague, now that they have made up and stopped quarrelling?
- What type of picture would be used, if the paper wanted to make us feel sorry for Romeo and Juliet?

After the play activities

Come and see the play: the greatest love story ever told!

Remember at the beginning, even before you read the play, you looked at the cover and tried to decide what the play would be about?
Now that you've read it, do the **symbols** make sense to you?

1 Use these or other **symbols** of your own to make up a poster that advertises the play.

Before you begin, answer these questions, because they will help you with the information you will need to put on the poster.

- What is the name of the play?
- What theatre will it be on at?
- What time will it begin?
- What dates will it be on at the theatre?
- What kind of play will it be, for example, a comedy or a tragedy?
- What words could describe the play, so that people will really want to see it?

Now that you have an idea of what you want to put on the poster, think again about the **symbols** you want to draw. Think about the **colours** you want to use.

2 When you have drawn your poster, write down why you chose to use special colours and symbols.

3 Show it to the rest of the class and tell them about its colours, its symbols and the information on it.
What did they think of your ideas?

Remember, you need to listen to other opinions, because they help you to **evaluate** your work and improve it.
You could display the posters so the whole class can look at the ideas.

© HODDER & STOUGHTON LTD 1999.
Copying permitted in purchasing school only.

After the play activities

Sort out the jumble!

Below you'll find some facts about the play *Romeo and Juliet*.
What you have to do is fill in the missing words. But that's not all.

The first letter of every answer is part of the name of a character in the play.
You have to find the answers, write down the letters, and then sort them out so that you come up with the name of the character.

1 After Romeo killed Tybalt, the Prince sent him into _____.
2 Friar _____ knew a lot about plants and herbs.
3 It was very _____ in the morning when the bodies of Romeo and Juliet were found.
4 Lord Montague was an _____ to Benvolio.
5 Romeo thought that he was _____ love with Rosaline.
6 The plague stopped Friar _____ from delivering the letter to Romeo in Mantua.
7 Lord Capulet said that the wedding would be on _____, before he changed his mind and made it Wednesday.
8 When Romeo was in the orchard, he saw Juliet and he stood _____ the balcony to talk to her.
9 The _____ was the bird that woke up Romeo and Juliet.
10 _____ murdered Mercutio.
11 The _____ was the most important man in Verona, and he wanted no more trouble from his people.
12 The party, where Romeo met Juliet, was at the _____ house.
13 Romeo went to buy his poison from an _____.

After the play activities

Writing horoscopes

Have you ever read your '**stars**' in a magazine or newspaper? Not everybody takes notice of them, but the **stars** play a big part in this play. Romeo and Juliet are '**star-cross'd lovers**'.

1 Match the horoscopes below with three characters.

2 Then, write one each for Romeo, Juliet and one other character before the play begins.

The week ahead

Decisions

This week you will have one of the hardest decisions of your life to make. You are asked for advice. Make sure you do the right thing, but beware – if things go wrong, be prepared to tell the truth.

Help

Someone very young and very close to you will need lots of help and support. You might not think that you can do much, because you are suffering too. But, if you don't help, you will lose that person.

Trouble

All you seem to do this week is try to keep the peace between friends and enemies. In fact, your help is needed to cheer up a close friend. Be ready for trouble and heartache, because people won't listen to you and you end up very upset indeed.

After the play activities

Good evening and welcome!

You have probably heard this at the beginning of a chat show!

Now it's your turn to **host** a chat show. You will be the person who welcomes your guest and you will ask the questions.

Your guest is going to be Juliet's Nurse.

1 Decide the title of your chat show, and then think of the questions you would like to ask the Nurse.

A few have been suggested, but you must come up with others.

- Why did you think so much of Juliet?
- What did you think of her marrying Romeo?
- Why did you help them, when you knew that the Capulets would have been so mad if they had found out?
- Do you think their marriage would have lasted if things hadn't gone so wrong?
- How did you feel when Tybalt was murdered? Did it affect Lady Capulet badly?

2 Once you have done this on your own, work with a partner.
Put your ideas together and decide on the final set of questions.

3 One of you must now take the part of the Nurse, and you must both work out what answers the Nurse would give to your questions.

4 Practise your chat show interview and when you are pleased with it, show it to the rest of your class. If you can book a video camera or a tape recorder, you might want to film or tape it, to see what it looks and sounds like.

After the play activities

If only . . .

If only . . . two words that show how easily the whole play might have been changed.

1 Read the sentences below. They have been split up, so that the beginning does not fit the rest of the sentence.

2 Find the correct fit, so that the sentences make sense.

If only . . .

a Rosaline .... hadn't met Romeo and asked him if he could read.
b Capulet's servant .... had managed to keep the peace.
c Romeo .... had agreed to love Romeo.
d Friar Laurence .... hadn't wanted Juliet to marry Paris.
e Mercutio .... had got through to Mantua with the letter.
f Friar John .... had woken up earlier.
g Capulet .... hadn't gone looking for Romeo.
h Tybalt .... had seen the signs of life in Juliet.
i Juliet .... hadn't picked a fight with Tybalt.
j Benvolio .... had given the letter to Balthasar and not to Friar John.

3 What do you think would have been Romeo's biggest regret?

After the play activities

Who is to blame?

There are so many people we can blame in this play.

1 Write down the names of the characters you could blame!

Did you come up with:
Capulet, Lady Capulet, Montague, Lady Montague, Nurse, Friar Laurence, Mercutio, Tybalt, Romeo, Juliet.
Is there anyone else you blame?

2 Write a sentence on each of these characters, explaining why you think they are to blame.

Lady Montague has already been done for you.

Lady Montague could be to blame, because she could have tried to persuade her husband to stop the fighting, by going to Capulet and trying to talk and make peace.

Now try your own sentences.
Once you have finished them show your ideas to a partner.

3 Out of ALL the characters, decide which ones are MOST to blame.

4 Once you have done this, decide how they should be punished. You need to give reasons for your decisions.

In the beginning, the Prince said that both Capulet and Montague would lose their lives if any more trouble broke out. Do you think they should still be punished by losing their lives?

Write down your thoughts, then read them to yourself. Check they make sense and that you have got reasons for what you say.

5 Now read your ideas to the class. See if they agree with you or have very different ideas.

After the play activities

So you want to be a star?

There must be lots of people who want to be on stage. They might even have an **ambition** to act in one of Shakespeare's plays.

1 If you had to play a character in the play *Romeo and Juliet*, which one would it be?

2 Once you have decided which part you want to play, explain why you chose that part.

3 Now look at one of your favourite scenes – it has to be one where you play the part you have chosen.
Think about the following and make notes:

- the costume you would wear in this scene – draw it if you can, but you must describe it, the colours, the design etc.
- the way your hair will be, any extra jewellery
- make-up
- what you will carry
- how you will walk on to stage and how you will say your words.

Remember that you have to show the audience what type of character you are through EVERYTHING about you – from the way you LOOK to the way you SPEAK!

4 Find out who has also chosen this character to play. Share your ideas with them.
What was different about your ideas? Did you come up with a few similar ideas?
Tell the rest of the class what you decided to do with your character.

After the play activities

Time waits for no man!

You have heard this said before. You might also have heard people say 'You can't turn back the clock'.
This is true of *Romeo and Juliet*.
It all happens in under a week!

Sunday: takes us up to the balcony scene.
Monday: takes us up to the night that Romeo spends with Juliet.
Tuesday: takes us up to Juliet taking the poison given to her by the Friar.
Wednesday: takes us up to Romeo stabbing himself in the vault and Juliet waking up to ...
Thursday just before dawn: Juliet stabs herself.

If we look closely, we might see that the time is not exactly right, but nobody watching the play would really notice.

1 Now answer these questions. Reading the information above will help you with the answers:

- On what day was the Capulet party?
- On what day did Romeo and Juliet get married?
- When did Romeo kill Tybalt?
- When did Juliet drink the poison?
- When was Juliet put in the vault?
- When did Romeo kill Paris?
- Does the play end on Thursday or Friday?

Which ever day it ends on, the most important idea is that everything happens so fast!

2 Think of reasons why Shakespeare wanted to make the action so fast. When you have come up with answers, share them with the class.

3 Imagine that someone says to you, 'Romeo and Juliet? There's not much action in that! It's about two lovers who die, that's all'
NOW what would you say to that person?!

IMPROVING PERFORMANCE IN PRIMARY SCHOOLS

Easy-to-use proformas for whole-school development and self-evaluation

Kevin Bullock

© Kevin Bullock 2005

Original edition published by pfp, ISBN 0-904677-06-1
New edition, published by Optimus Education, 2007, ISBN 978-1-905538-41-6

All rights reserved. No part of this publication may be reproduced, stored in a retrieval system, or transmitted in any form or by any means, electronic, mechanical, photocopying, recording or otherwise without the permission of the publisher.

Applications for reproduction should be made in writing to
Optimus Education, 33-41 Dallington Street, London EC1V 0BB.

The information contained in this publication is believed to be correct at the time of going to press. Whilst care has been taken to ensure that the information is accurate, the publisher can accept no responsibility for any errors or omissions or for changes to the details given.

A CIP catalogue record for this book is available from the British Library.

Printed in England by:
Piggott Black Bear
The Paddocks
Cherry Hinton Road
Cambridge CB1 8DH
Tel: 01223 424571

Designed by:
Character Design
Highridge
Lower Wrigglebrook Lane
Kingsthorne
Hereford HR2 8AW
Tel: 01981 541154

Published by Optimus Education, a trading name of Optimus Professional Publishing Ltd, Registered Office 33-41 Dallington Street, London EC1V 0BB. Registered in England and Wales. Registered no. 05791519.

IMPROVING PERFORMANCE IN PRIMARY SCHOOLS

Easy-to-use proformas for whole-school development and self-evaluation

Kevin Bullock

Contents

Foreword 1
Getting to know the proformas 2
Sample proformas 3
Q&A 13
Introducing the proformas 15
Using the proformas 16
Managing the proformas 19
At a glance – Overview of proformas 20
Proforma tracking sheet 21
Step by step through the proformas 23

Section 1:
Proformas that monitor pupils' work and progress 23

Section 2:
Proformas that assist subject coordinators in their role . 24

Section 3:
Proformas that assist with whole-school strategic planning 24

Section 4:
Proformas that assist with collating performance information 25

Proformas 1-9
Monitoring pupils' work and progress 27
Proforma 1: Monitoring and presenting pupils' work 28
Proforma 2: Monitoring basic skills with inclusivity in mind 30
Proforma 3: Whole-school monitoring 32
Proforma 4: Work sampling 34
Proforma 5: Subject report evaluation sheet 36
Proforma 6: Class survey 38
Proforma 7: Expectation sheet 40
Proforma 8: Attitude/progress sheet 42
Proforma 9: SATs predictions 44

Proformas 10-14

Assisting the subject coordinators in their role **47**

Proforma 10: Subject coordinators' checklist 48

Proforma 11: Subject coordinators' summary of monitoring 50

Proforma 12: Improving standards 52

Proforma 13: Self-appraisal for subject coordinators 54

Proforma 14: My personal development planning sheet 56

Proformas 15-20

Whole-school strategic planning **59**

Proforma 15: Strategies for monitoring educational standards 60

Proforma 16: Subject priorities 62

Proforma 17: Teacher appraisal/monitoring 64

Proforma 18: Teaching and learning observations 66

Proforma 19: Governing body 68

Proforma 20: School development 70

Proformas 21-24

Collating performance information **73**

Proformas 21 and 22: Prompting sentences 74

Proforma 23: Continuous professional development for teachers 76

Proforma 24: Summary of CPD for individual teachers 78

Proformas 25-27

Performance management **82**

Proforma 25: The review meeting 83

Proforma 26: The planning statement/s 84

Proforma 27: The objectives 85

Further reading **86**

Foreword

The emphasis on modern school inspection is embedded in self-evaluation.

> *Ofsted believes that schools are best placed to recognise their own strengths and weaknesses. This is why we are introducing a new inspection system which puts more onus on a school to be proactive and demonstrate to inspectors that it can not only diagnose where its strengths and weaknesses are, but more crucially, do something about improving and developing them.*
>
> (**www.ofsted.gov.uk/ofsteddirect** re: Self-evaluation and the self-evaluation form)

The proformas in this pack encourage **self-evaluation** – at **all** levels. As headteacher, you will be able to collate, through your staff, a wealth of robust self-evaluation information. Your teaching staff will have an easy-to-use process for evaluating their own teaching, and their pupils' learning, both as class teachers and as subject coordinators. All staff members will have a process for evaluating their own professional development. Governors and other stakeholders can contribute to the information you have about the school, by following the key questions in the proformas.

The proformas are designed to encourage **curriculum leadership** at all levels – a key Ofsted focus, and **continuous professional development** for all teachers – a major part of the government's *Excellence and Enjoyment* initiative.

The information you will gather when using these proformas will form a powerful tool in future Ofsted inspections, but more importantly, in your ongoing school improvement. This pack provides a framework that penetrates to the core of **teaching and learning**, enabling you, along with your school management team and your teachers, to focus more clearly on the pertinent issues:

Standards **A**chievement **L**earning **T**eaching

– the **SALT** of education.

The proformas are designed so that each aspect of information gathered can be fed back into whole-school development plans with ease. They provide a simple trail from class teaching to whole-school improvement and back again. The procedures are fast, robust and accurate. You can exchange the pastime of stumbling through stifling policies for directing and driving streamlined proformas. The valuable time saved in meetings, staff appraisals and school improvement reports will allow you space and energy to focus on the vision and direction of your school.

Throughout this pack the main aim is to keep **The Main Aim** as the main aim: in other words to allow you to concentrate on improving the teaching and learning in your school.

The term 'subject coordinator' has been used throughout the proformas – you can substitute this for 'subject leader', 'line manager' or whatever term is preferred in your school.

Getting to know the proformas

The proformas come in two styles:
- some provide advice for staff as they undertake evaluation procedures
- some are for completion.

All of them are accessible on the accompanying CD-Rom, so that you can modify them to suit your own school, add your school name, increase the size of boxes and so on.

Take time to familiarise yourself with these proformas before you try to introduce them to your staff. Pages 4 to 12 show some of the proformas filled in: look at these, alongside the master copies.

There are 27 proformas in all, covering a variety of activities and tasks. Some cover basic information while others are more complex. To a greater or lesser degree they are all interrelated, yet can be used in isolation when required.

The proformas are divided into five sections:
- monitoring pupils' work and progress (proformas 1 – 9)
- assisting the subject coordinators in their role (proformas 10 – 14)
- whole-school strategic planning (proformas 15 – 20)
- collating performance information (proformas 21 – 24)
- performance management.

Together these cover all aspects of school improvement work in a simple and straightforward format.

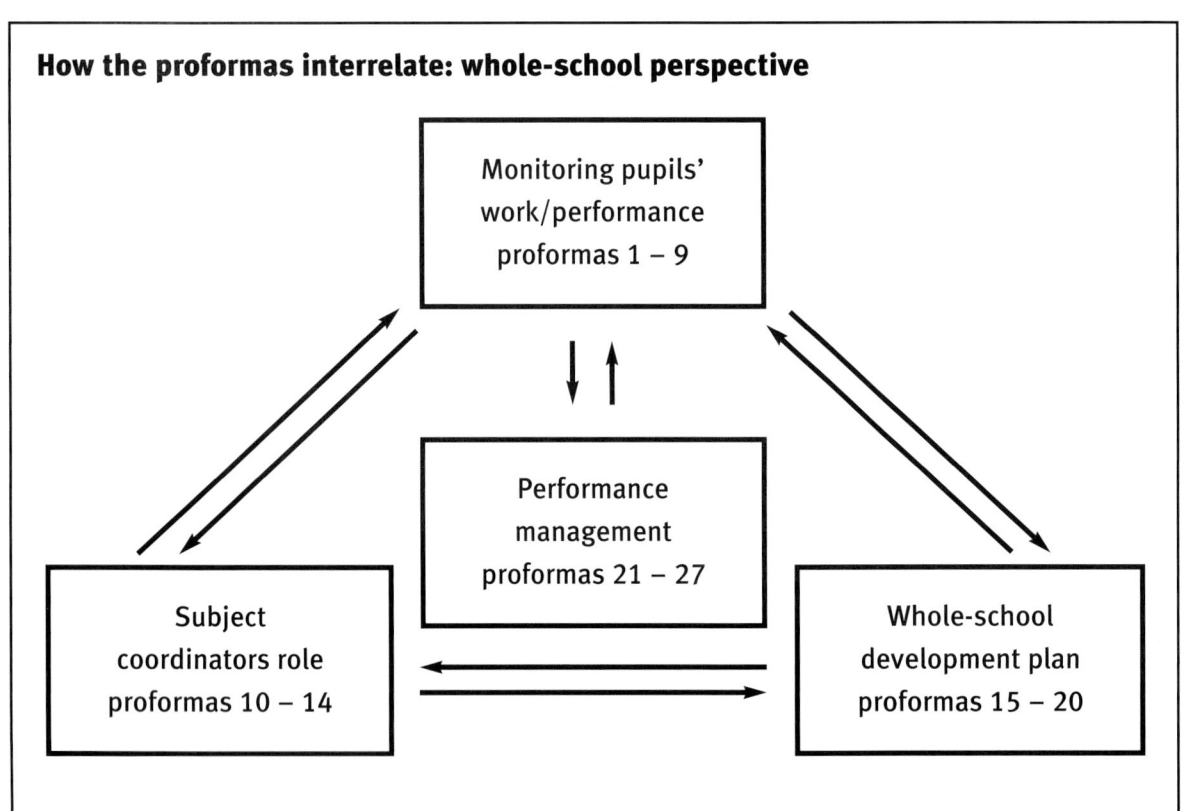

Accompanying each proforma is a guidance sheet. This provides information about:
- the intended objective/s
- links with the whole-school development cycle
- the key personnel for whom it is designed
- how it might contribute to whole-school improvement
- the next steps to take.

Read this information carefully, as it will help you to think about the most appropriate proforma to use to gather specific information about your school.

The important thing is to make the proformas work for you, with your staff and in your particular situation. This pack is versatile. It can be used to shape practice, highlight gaps and ensure a consistent approach in a variety of contexts. It is for you to decide how it can best be deployed in your school.

> *'All inspection findings must be rooted in evidence.*
> *The most valuable and informative evidence is that obtained first hand...'*
>
> *(Ofsted Handbook, 2003)*

Ofsted highlights a hierarchical evidence base, of which the most valuable and informative are:
- observations/evidence of learning
- pupils' work/talking to pupils
- talking to staff/analysing performance indicators
- evaluating school processes in supporting/reinforcing the above.

The proformas are based on this premise.

Sample proformas

Please see overleaf for an illustration of how proformas can be cross-referenced.

'School development' proforma (20) is the starting point.

(20) School development

Priority
English SATs results in 2008

Target
To ensure we achieve 92% at L4 in the above test

Success criteria
92% is achieved in English in 2008

Task/s
Take stock of current standards – Expectation sheet, proforma 7
Transfer data onto SATs predictions sheet, proforma 9
Gain insight into pupil attitude/achievement perceptions via Attitude/progress sheet, proforma 8
Subject coordinator to complete improving standards report, based on above information – proforma 12
Line manager to support/direct subject coordinator via Personal development planning, proforma 14

Time scale	**Personnel**	**Resources**
Jan 07 – Summer 08	*Subject coordinator* *Line manager* *Class teacher*	*Non-contact time*
Monitoring and review	**Evaluation**	**Miscellaneous notes**
All monitoring info to be shared with teaching assistant. *Monitoring meeting monthly with line manager.*	*To take place after results in 2008 are known – Teacher* *Subject coordinator* *Line manager* *Headteacher*	*Also use Work sampling proforma 4* *In conjunction with Attitude/progress proforma 8*

(7) Expectation sheet

Class .... *Mr Unknown* .... Year .... *Year 5* ....

Children working below their expected level in *English*

a) Slightly below
   Pupils   1, 7, 9, 15, 21   *(5 pupils)*

b) Below
   Pupils   6, 7   *(2 pupils)*

c) Substantially below
   Pupils   4, 22   *(2 pupils)*

Strategies to counter underachievement

Extra homework classes

Booster classes

Closer class monitoring of a + b pupils above

No. in class *30 (each child = 3.3%)*   **Usual time of lesson** *9:15 – 10:15*

Calculations

If A achieve   =   *21 + 5 = 26 pupils = 86%*

If B achieve   =   *21 + 7 = 28 = 92%*

If C achieve   =   *As there are a total of 9 pupils currently working below the expected level for this age we have 21 out of 30 who should achieve level 4.*

21 × 3.3% = 69%

To hit our target it is vital that both a + b pupils come up to expected level.

(9) SATs predictions

Name of teacher (current and previous) *Mrs ex-teacher, Mr Unknown*		
Year 2 SATs	**Year 6 SATs** ✓	**Results**
Percentage achieving Level ......4......... in		
Subject	**Best case scenario**	**Worst case scenario**
English ✓	*92%*	*69%*
Mathematics		
Science		

Related information	
No. IEPs	*3*
Previous: QCA optional SATs results	*See data with teacher but many pupils appear to have slipped back*
Relevant in-house test information	*See in-house reading tests data – again some slipped*
Teacher assessment/evidence	*Samples of work ready for analysis*
Baseline assessment or otherwise	*N/A*

Comments
The above best case scenario is dependent upon both slightly below and below expected level pupils achieving at expected level (see proforma 7).

(8) Attitude/progress sheet

Subject .... *English* .... Year ....

Date .... *Jan 21st* .... Name .... *Pupil X* ....

	Poor				Excellent
Confidence	1	(2)	3	4	5
Motivation	1	(2)	3	4	5
Listening	1	2	(3)	4	5
Communication	1	2	(3)	4	5

Effort	Achievement	Trend
A	A	**Improving**
B	B	
C	(C)	**Steady**
(D)	D	
E	E	**(More application needed)**

Comments

Pupil X is lacking both confidence and motivation, this in turn is having an effect on effort and achievement. As many of the pupils in this class scored low on motivation, I believe motivation is the key to improvement. It appears that the low confidence score is a result of low motivation and not the other way around.

(8) Attitude/progress sheet

Subject ..... *English* ..... Year ....

Date ..... *Jan 21st* ..... Name ..... *Pupil Y* .....

	Poor				Excellent
Confidence	1	2	3	(4)	5
Motivation	1	(2)	3	4	5
Listening	1	2	(3)	4	5
Communication	1	2	(3)	4	5

Effort	Achievement	Trend
A	A	**Improving**
B	B	
(C)	C	**Steady**
D	(D)	
E	E	**(More application needed)**

Comments

Pupil Y is not the only pupil to score high on the confidence scale yet low on the motivation. I therefore believe motivation is a key factor in the lack of progress seen of late in this class.

(12) Improving standards

Improving standards in .... *English* .... (subject)

Brief report

Current standards/achievement (including specific cohorts of pupils year/key stage groups, etc.)

Current standards are low.

Progress has stalled.

Motivation appears to be a key factor in improving the situation.

Recent development work and how this has improved standards

N/A

Future development work and how this will improve standards

A sharp focus on teaching and learning in the classroom to ascertain why there is a lack of motivation.

In-depth chats to pupils to expand on why they're not motivated.

Monitoring meetings to evaluate progress on a monthly basis.

Robust work samples in English.

Extra booster classes.

Closer scrutiny of pupils' progress working below and slightly below expected level.

Other comments

Use 'My personal development planning sheet', proforma 14, to focus both on the subject coordinator's and class teacher's development.

(4) Work sampling

Three pupils from appropriate class/es working at above average standard, average standard, below average standard and any other relevant category bring work with them.

General questions might include

- What did you really enjoy doing?
- Why?
- Tell me about some of the things that you have learned.
- How do you think you are getting on in...?
- What didn't you enjoy doing?
- What things did you find most difficult?
- Why? Etc.

Focus also on specific pieces of work and ask them to tell you about how/why/when they did it, etc.

Other possible questions

Ask the pupil open questions that will give an insight into the apparent lack of motivation/confidence.

Get the pupil to talk about a piece of completed work of which they are really proud. What were the key factors that contributed to this success?

Ask questions that may shed some light on their peers' attitude towards class work (negative or otherwise).

Ask the pupil what would actually encourage them to work consistently harder.

(14) My personal development planning sheet — Class teacher

Priority

To motivate the significant number of 'switched-off' pupils.

Target

To ensure 92% of my class is working within the expected level for Year 4 pupils.

Success criteria

(see above) Are they?

Tasks

Modifying teaching and learning to motivate all pupils.

Modifying teaching and learning to improve pupil performance.

Time scale

July 08

Personnel to support me

Line manager

Resources I will need

To be discussed when line manager observes teaching and learning next week.

Peer support.

Monitoring review – how/who?

See proforma 12.

Evaluation

Miscellaneous notes

(14) My personal development planning sheet — Line manager

Priority

To support and direct class teacher as she modifies her teaching and learning in an attempt to re-motivate pupils.

Target

To ensure 92% of her class is working within the expected level for Year 4 pupils.

Success criteria

(see above) Are they?

Tasks

To support and direct teacher so that teaching and learning motivate all pupils.
To support and direct teacher in improving pupil performance.

Time scale

July 08

Personnel to support me

Headteacher

Resources I will need

To finalise after teaching and learning has been observed next week.

Monitoring review – how/who?

See proforma 12.

Evaluation

Miscellaneous notes

Q&A

What's the secret of the proformas' effectiveness?

Simply using tried-and-tested proformas to streamline communication, clarify key issues and focus directly on teaching and learning.

What if I have limited ICT skills?

There is no need to incorporate ICT with this pack. In fact, the sharing and passing on of handwritten proformas is as effective and seamless as many programs currently on the market.

What benefits will my school gain from using this pack?

- Every stakeholder in your school will feel they have a voice through completing one or more versions of the central 'School development' proforma (20), which identifies school priorities for improvement.
- The school will gain a broad view of priorities, taking account of the viewpoints of the different stakeholders.
- If all proformas are given out and returned within, say, 72 hours, you will have a framework for a comprehensive school development plan in just three days.
- The two whole-school development proformas can save hours of meetings and report writing.
- When the governor input grid has been incorporated into the sections of school development it can greatly enhance communication and problem solving.
- The school development proforma will revolutionise the way you keep abreast of school development, organisation and bureaucracy.

That may be the case, but won't prioritising the issues be a nightmare?

Prioritising will simply be about deciding into which of three piles you place the individual proformas: A, B or C.

A = Action (now)   B = Brewing   C = Coming up

The headteacher may make three tentative piles, but then through discussion with staff, governors and other stakeholders, the piles might be modified. The advantage to this procedure is that nothing is set in stone and you're not lumbered with an outdated document after a couple of months.

How do you incorporate the other proformas?

'School development' proforma (20) can be cross-referenced with any number of other proformas depending on the actual priority, and the amount of further information you require. Throughout this pack you will be guided to potential cross-referencing opportunities in the guidance sheets accompanying each proforma.

How will this help transform my leadership style?

This pack is a management tool. Using it will enable you to streamline the management of your school's development. These proformas will keep personnel on-task, leading them through the process of evaluating the performance of your school. With this taken care of, you will be released for the vital headship role of clear directional and strategic leadership. Remember, management is all about doing things right, while transformational leadership is all about doing the right things.

Effective leaders work on their indirect influence. They realise they can't split themselves into a dozen parts, but need to know that their staff are focused in their absence.

You can't be everywhere at once – but the proformas can!

Introducing the proformas

Once you are familiar with the proformas and how they can benefit your school, you need to decide how to share this with the rest of your staff and your governors.

Decide on a launch day, possibly a professional development day, and introduce your staff to the proformas and guidance.

- Photocopy the pack so that each proforma and its guidance notes are on a single A3 sheet.
- Provide each member of staff with a reference grid, with the proforma numbers and titles down the left hand side. Space on the right can be used for notes.

Allow time for staff to look through the material and familiarise themselves with the general layout. You could approach this in different ways:

- Whole packs could be spread out on tables and the staff could sit round in their key stage or year groups and discuss the proformas.
- Put one section of proformas, clearly labelled, on each of four large tables, one section per table, and allow staff to move round them in their own time.

You can then make a more formal presentation, introducing the proformas and how you intend that they should be used. It might be helpful if you have talked this through with your senior management team or other key staff first, so that they can support you in your presentation.

Introduce the system to your governors by explaining the process to them, explaining what is entailed and the benefits as you see them. Show them examples of the proformas and the accompanying guidance. Spend more time on the governors' proforma (19) and the school development proforma (20), explaining how these will improve your current approach to whole-school development.

There are alternative ways to use these proformas.

- **Cherry picking:** simply select a handful of proformas that would fill the gaps in your school's improvement programme and try them out. Modify them to fit the context of your own school and ask for feedback on their effectiveness. In short, select, trial and review a handful at a time.
- **Delegating choice:** this option gives your staff the initial responsibility for selecting the proformas to use within their own practice. As schools choose their own procedures for self-evaluation, so do individual teachers. Teachers are given copies of the whole pack and even granted professional development time to become familiar with aspects of it. They are then left to implement various categories into their own practice. It is likely that different individuals will have preferences for different proformas. After one or two terms organise whole-school feedback and evaluation to ascertain which proformas are the most popular and the most useful, and which are the least favoured. This in itself will give a good insight into school improvement issues.

Using the proformas

Like all planning, managing the performance of your school, in all its aspects, is a cyclical affair. To start the process you have to break into that cycle at some point. Once you have done this and set the ball rolling it will continue.

The whole pack centres on proforma 20, 'School development', so this is the point at which you could start the cycle for your school.

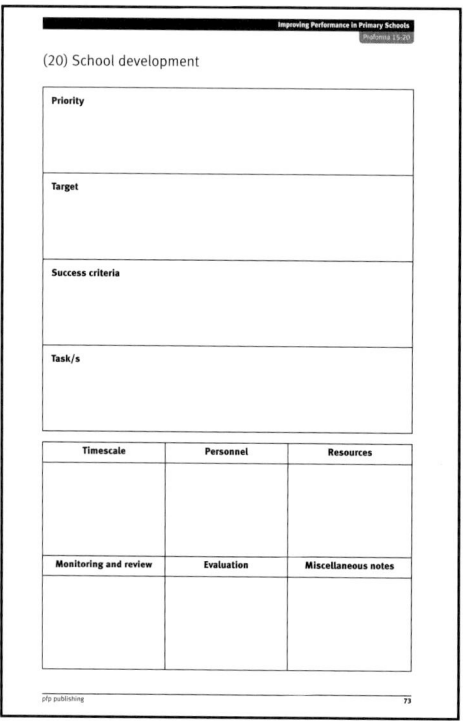

The headings will be familiar to you, even if the layout is new. This proforma is both the entry and the exit point for all your school development planning. The information gathered on all the other forms will eventually be reflected in it.

Distribute proforma 20

Make copies of proforma 20 and give one to each stakeholder: your staff (teachers, teaching assistants, PAs, cleaners, midday supervisors and so on), a representative sample of pupils and the governors. Ask them to fill in the first section, 'Priority', and return it to you within, say, 72 hours. Making this activity accessible to all empowers people, and the simplicity of the layout helps everyone to be able to contribute.

Alternatively, invite governors and other adult stakeholders to join teaching staff on a professional development day. Hand out copies of proforma 20 to each individual, ask them to complete the first section focusing on their own particular responsibilities. Spend the rest of the day deciding on the priorities and then detailing the tasks, etc. (see the following sections) and you can have your whole-school development plan completed in one day.

Once you have all the returned proformas, you will be able to finalise details and prioritise the issues.

Prioritise the priorities

Do this by setting up three piles.

Pile A	Pile B	Pile C
Action – now	Brewing	Coming up

These categories will represent issues that are of high, medium or low priority for your school at this point. The most challenging part of this process is deciding what goes into the school development plan (pile A), what goes into the reserve list (pile B) and what stops on its original pile (pile C).

Make three tentative piles yourself (having removed any duplicate priorities first), and then in discussion with staff, governors and other stakeholders, modify them. Decisions necessarily have to be context-based and evaluated by appropriate personnel.

The advantage of this procedure is that nothing is fixed, so it's easy to make changes now and 'unchange' them if necessary at some later date. You can easily re-categorise your priorities, up-grading or down-grading issues as school priorities change, as the result of the findings of an Ofsted inspection, as you realise through further self-evaluation that there is a more serious issue to be tackled, or in response to a changing government initiative. Because your priorities can be changed easily you will be willing to make those changes. There's nothing more annoying than having put it all into one document, taking hours of your time and the PA's time only to find that you need to make changes, and that means changing the whole thing – a daunting process that may cause you to react by ignoring it altogether. With this system you simply shuffle those papers and change the contents of your three piles.

Completing the proformas

If this is your first cycle you may need to pause at this point in order to collate more information, either by using other proformas from this pack or transferring information you already have. In future years you should have the information available.

The first section, 'Priority', will already be filled in.

The next two sections, 'Target' and 'Success criteria', will be familiar to you. 'Target' should be based on facts, not a notion or figure plucked from the air. There are proformas within the pack that will help you with this. 'Success criteria' should be measurable.

The fourth section is 'Tasks'; this section may include different information dependent upon the priority you have identified. It may be that there is a perceived problem or area for development identified in the priority section. You then need to collect the relevant data, in which case you will be listing the proformas to be used for this in the task section. Once you have this data you may decide that the priority as stated can in fact wait to be dealt with, and this proforma 20 can be moved to pile B or even pile C. It may be that the evidence proves the need for further action, in which case a new proforma 20 can be filled in. The task section will then include specific actions that staff will be taking to address the issue.

Alternatively, the priority may have been set because of the data you already have. In this case the proforma 20 will list the actions to be taken to address the issue.

Of course, a third option is that you will need a mixture of the two: proformas for further evidence and tasks, and maybe proformas to measure the level of success at the end of the process.

The remaining six boxes are self evident, but look at the sample proforma 20 on page 4 for more details.

Cross-referencing

If you look at the examples of completed proformas, pages 4 to 12, you will see how proformas can be cross-referenced.

In this particular example, the tasks are concerned primarily with completing other proformas to find out why results are low, and how they can be raised. So the relevant proformas are listed in the 'Tasks' section. (In the 'Personnel' section you could identify by number which proformas are to be completed by which section of personnel.) Having found out this information you may decide to complete another proforma 20, with the actions you need to take to address the issues raised by the information.

In some instances, the tasks will cover other actions that might be taken, and the proformas that hold the information leading to the identifying of the priority will then be listed in the monitoring and review section of proforma 20.

For other proformas there are suggestions for cross-referencing in the guide sheets.

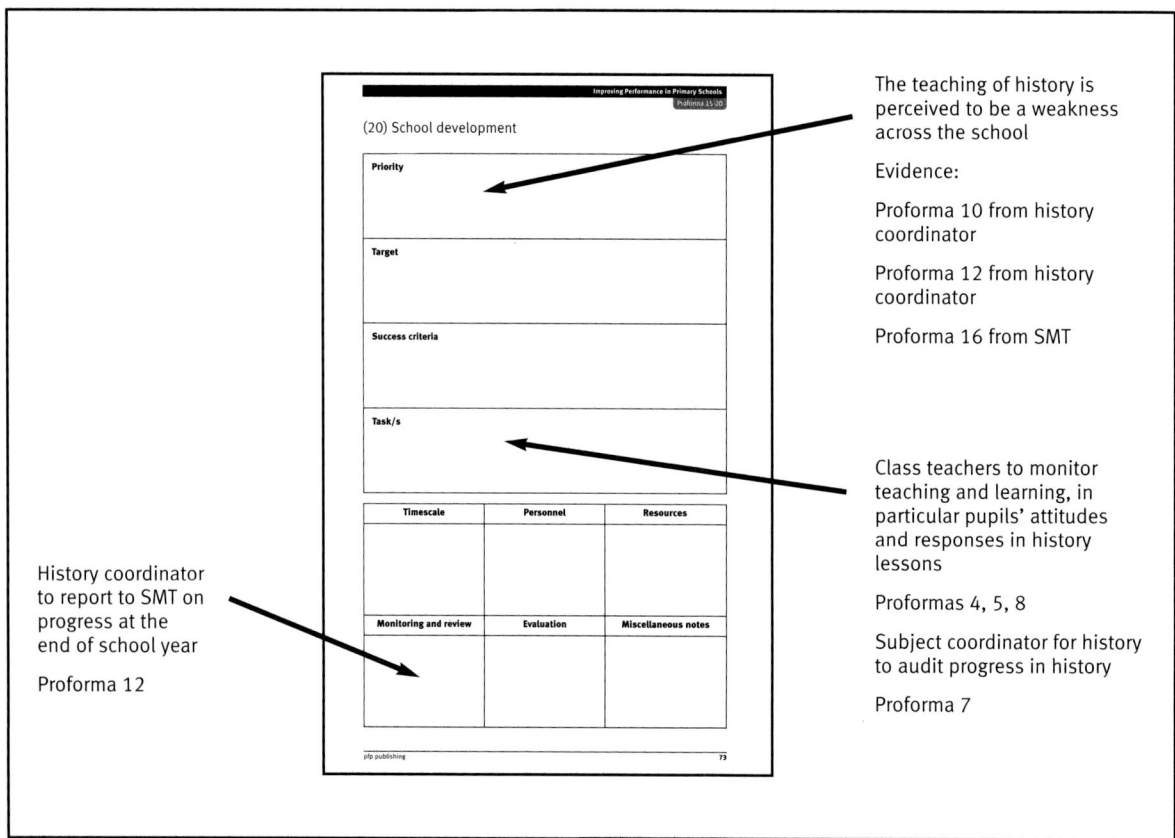

This is only one example of how varying proformas can link together to aid joined-up thinking. Any permutation is of course possible, depending on the priority and context.

Managing the proformas

Before you start to distribute proformas to your staff and stakeholders it is useful to spend some time thinking about how you will manage the many sheets of paper you could end up with. It is important that the information you store is accessible.

A key task is the storing and collating of information when copies of the proformas are returned to you. You need to set up a school improvement filing system covering the broad categories of this pack. Box files, drawer file units and suchlike are ideal. The proforma categorisation will be down to your own preference and reflect the context of your own school. Whatever system you decide upon, prepare it, or ask your PA to do this, before you introduce the pack to your staff. They need to know where everything is going to be stored.

Sorting out a storage system will help to clarify in your mind the way in which different proformas will impact on other proformas, on which ones will be used by other personnel within the school, which will be kept by class teachers or handed to senior staff and so on. Will you need a central system that all can access? If everything is kept in your office, who can access it? Which parts can be discarded and shredded once the information has been passed on or absorbed into another proforma?

Master copies of the proformas that you have decided class teachers will use, and their accompanying guidance sheets, should be prepared and stored for anyone to make their own copies as and when they need them.

Sometimes you will be distributing proformas to various members of your staff or your stakeholders. On page 21 you will find a sheet that you or a senior member of staff can use to track these. It will assist you to remember who is completing what, and by when. This is also evidence of the ongoing self-evaluation within your school, and as such is a document worth keeping.

You may need a perception shift within your school concerning whole-school improvement planning. Talking with your staff about the best ways to store and manage the data might lead naturally into this discussion. Discuss some of these statements with your staff and governors. It will help them to see the rationale of this new approach.

- The old system was neat because everything was in one easily-stored file.
- The information in the old file was quickly out of date.
- It was difficult to add to or change anything in the old file if a new priority arose.
- This material can be easily duplicated.
- Everyone can access the proformas and so contribute to the programme of managing improvement.
- Old style plans could slow down improvement due to their static and inaccessible nature.
- Information can be updated immediately.
- Information is easy to cross-reference.

Should files be the tail that wags the educational dog, or should continually improving practice dictate the rhythm and direction of the paperwork?

At a glance

Overview of proformas

1 Monitoring and presenting pupils' work 2 Monitoring basic skills with inclusivity in mind 3 Whole-school monitoring 4 Work sampling 5 Subject report evaluation sheet 6 Class survey 7 Expectation sheet 8 Attitude/progress sheet 9 SATs predictions sheet	**Monitoring pupils' work and progress** For itemised proformas see page 23
10 Subject coordinators' checklist 11 Subject coordinators' summary of monitoring 12 Improving standards 13 Self-appraisal for subject coordinators 14 My personal development planning sheet	**Assisting the subject coordinators in their role** For itemised proformas see page 24
15 Strategies for monitoring educational standards 16 Subject priorities 17 Teacher appraisal/monitoring 18 Teaching and learning observations 19 Governing body 20 School development	**Whole-school strategic planning** For itemised proformas see page 24 • Overall objectives • Monitoring • Teaching and learning • Whole-school development
21 Prompting sentences – Sheet 1 and 2 23 Continuous professional development for teachers 24 CPD for individual teachers	**Collating performance information** For itemised proformas see page 25
25 The review meeting 26 The planning statement 27 The objectives	**Performance management** For itemised proformas see page 26

Proforma tracking sheet

Nos		Given to name/s	Date	Return date
	Monitoring pupils' work			
	Subject coordinators' roles			
	Whole-school strategic planning			
	Performance management			
Nos		Given to name/s	Date	Return date

When Ofsted or other inspectors, or your governors want to know about your school improvement planning or your self-evaluation you can hand them a copy of the diagram on page 20: 'Overview of proformas'. They can then mark the ones which they will find useful and you can remove the appropriate files containing those specific proformas from your filing system. Completed forms will indicate any cross-referenced information and they can access this too if they so wish.

On the occasions that a written report on school development issues is required, information is simply lifted off the appropriate part of the proformas. The days of keeping a school development folder up to date and/or re-writing a new one every one, two or three years are over!

Step by step through the proformas

The following 27 proformas have been developed with both school inspection and school improvement in mind. They are tried and tested and have been effective in improving both standards and performance. In short they:

- focus on the important aspects of headship, teaching and learning
- support staff in self-assessment and further development so they are self-reliant with regard to future direction
- save valuable time thumbing through policy and handbooks – the proformas cover all areas of teaching and learning
- enhance joined-up thinking, teamwork and include all people at all levels
- revolutionise school development planning – no need for bulky folders which become outdated so quickly.

The proformas are divided into five sections

1. Monitoring pupils' work and progress
2. Assisting the subject coordinators in their role
3. Whole-school strategic planning
4. Collating performance information
4. Performance management

Section 1:

Proformas that monitor pupils' work and progress

Can be used by headteacher, subject coordinator and class teachers.

Overall objectives

1. To ensure focused monitoring and consistency in marking pupils' work.
   To remind teachers of some key learning information.
2. To clarify what we mean by inclusivity and raising questions to ensure that there is no under-achievement within the school.
3. To record the pupil groupings on a standardised form and highlight other key data about the grouping, so enabling an informative grouping profile to emerge.
4. To conduct effective work sampling by scrutinising above average, average and below average samples of pupils' work.
5. To obtain a written subject report from a pupil's perspective and additional personal information through interaction with the pupil.
6. To gauge the pupils' responses before the official letters and/or questionnaires are sent out at the time of the next Ofsted inspection.
7. To provide a class/year group expectation profile very quickly from which future target-setting data can be produced.
8. To provide an instant pupil profile snapshot covering effort, achievement and personal information.

9. To provide an instant snapshot (best and worst case scenarios) for SATs predictions in English, mathematics and science.

These proformas can be used individually or combined to inform the teacher, subject coordinator or headteacher on matters relating to the monitoring and progression of pupils' work. When the information has been recorded on the proformas they can be photocopied and handed on, or transferred to the appropriate subject coordinator proforma (see section 2) and fed into the overall school improvement plan. The subject coordinators' proformas can also assist the coordinator in identifying their own performance management goals and development needs (see section 4).

Section 2:

Proformas that assist subject coordinators in their role

Overall objectives

10. To provide the subject coordinators with a checklist to help prioritise their tasks.
11. To assist the coordinator in gaining an overview of what monitoring proformas are available and their reference numbers.
12. To provide a framework for a subject coordinator to write a report about standards in their subject.
13. To assist a subject coordinator in evaluating and reflecting on their current and future role/s.
14. To assist the member of staff in devising their own personal development plan.

Section 3:

Proformas that assist with whole-school strategic planning

These provide a common format on which to record all development areas/issues/concerns which are to emerge as the ongoing school improvement plan.

Of course, many of these proformas can be used by both teacher and subject coordinator.

Overall objectives

Monitoring

15. To give the sequence and overview of key tasks associated with key tools for school improvement.
16. To give an overview of subject teaching observations and the monitoring of work.

Teaching and learning

17. To assist the senior management team with the monitoring of individual teacher appraisal.
18. To help the lesson observer focus on key questions that relate to effective teaching and learning.

Whole-school development

19. To enable governors (or other stakeholders) to get to the core of a problem before raising it as a vague concern at a school meeting.

20. The central proforma for all priorities which links the others together.

The above proformas are set into three sections for convenience and ease of explanation. The categories, however, do overlap and should not be seen as relating to just one section. Each school should put their own interpretation on their use and modify them accordingly.

Also note that the above guides for lesson observations are not suggested as a replacement to existing observation sheets. Over the years many excellent literacy, numeracy and LEA observation sheets (including individual schools' in-house ones) have been devised. You should continue to use the forms that are most relevant and appropriate to your own particular context.

Section 4:

Proformas that assist with collating performance information

Overall objectives

21/22. Prompting sentences. This assists the teacher/subject coordinator in pulling everything together. Other proformas would have helped clarify strengths or weaknesses in both his or her own performance and his subject/s.

23. These questions were devised in order to encapsulate the key issues identified in producing effective teachers. This can be used by individuals as a self-assessment exercise or as part of performance management interview.

Update of professional development

24. Teachers are not always effective in recording their past professional development so this form is a constant reminder. It also reminds staff that visiting colleagues in other classes and/or schools or listening to an inspiring and knowledgeable speaker is all part of their professional development experience.

As a result of the professional development proforma, the teacher/subject coordinator may revisit the subject coordinator proformas, especially 14 – 'My personal development planning sheet' – to help plan his or her future direction.

Section 5:

Can be used by reviewer and reviewee

Overall objectives

Proformas that aid the performance management process

25. To give a format for agreeing objectives at the review meeting

26. To record the jointly agreed planning statement
27. To record the three or four objectives for the performance management cycle

Although performance management is the final part of this section, in reality, the whole process is cyclic and ongoing. All proformas can be incorporated simultaneously and/or in any order chosen by the individual schools.

If you want to see all of the proformas at a glance, there is a summary sheet on page 20. If you want to track the proformas you have distributed amongst your staff there is a tracking sheet on page 21.

Proformas 1-9

Monitoring pupils' work and progress

● Proforma 1: Monitoring and presenting pupils' work

Objective
To ensure focused monitoring and consistency in marking pupils' work.
To remind teachers of some key learning information.

This guidance sheet reminds the senior management team and teachers that there is a finite amount of time for marking pupils' work. It is therefore crucial from the outset to clarify and prioritise what will be assessed. Similarly, it releases the busy teacher from being tempted to mark everything.

The second part of the guidance sheet covers key learning issues and encourages the teacher to think about the different ways in which information might be presented to different pupils.

Links to school cycle
This guidance sheet can be introduced at the beginning of a new school year to ensure consistency and focus in whole-school marking. It can be used as a reference at different stages of the year to gauge marking coherence and consistency between teachers, year cohorts, and key stage groups. The guidance can also be used to promote staff discussion on important issues relating to marking and monitoring. This sheet will certainly help to clarify thinking prior to an inspection visit.

Likewise, the second half of the sheet, covering learning styles, can be deployed in a similar way.

Key personnel
Senior management team and/or subject coordinators can use this guidance as part of their whole-school work monitoring role.

In lesson observations, line managers can evaluate how teachers are modifying their teaching to cater for the varying learning styles within their classes.

How this contributes to school improvement
- Ensures whole-school consistency in monitoring pupils' work, a key Ofsted focus.
- Encourages teachers to cater for a variety of learning styles in their teaching.
- More focused marking.
- Sharper and smarter use of teachers' time.
- Encourages more individual learning.

Next steps
- Ensure all teachers adhere to all or part of the guidance.
- Publicise the marking rationale to parents.
- Include this information with other monitoring guidance.
- Begin to construct a learning style profile of all pupils at the school.

(1) Monitoring and presenting pupils' work – including marking guidance

If your objectives are clear then your marking focus will be straightforward. Simply
- identify where the objective/s has/have been achieved
- identify where to give further development/guidance/targets
- keep comments concise, constructive and clear
- a general comment on effort might be useful.

Marking should be strategic, ie. not every piece of work.
It does not have to be whole-class marking.
Oral feedback is more likely to inspire, motivate and clarify misunderstandings.

Encourage pupils to take ownership of future targets, don't let it become a bureaucratic exercise.

Remember, when presenting work, the implications of different learning styles and the difference between right/left brain functions.

Learning styles

The difference between right/left brain function.

	Left	**Right**
	Sequential – from part to whole	Whole picture first
Visual	Critical thinking	Emotion
Auditory	Logic	Space
Kinaesthetic	Analysis	Creativity
	Systems	Images

The brain works by association linking random concepts/ideas/facts into an interconnected network of knowledge. Mind mapping is a good strategy for clarifying concepts and extending ideas.

Remember

- most of the brain's capacity remains unused
- intelligence can be learned
- memory relies on meaning and patterns – the most effective way to learn something new is to see how it relates/builds upon something the child already knows
- emotions trigger in before intellect and can block or enhance learning
- self-motivation is a key to success
- our eating, drinking, exercise, sleeping and all other habits have a direct link on our ability to learn.

Proforma 2: Monitoring basic skills with inclusivity in mind

Objective

To clarify what we mean by inclusivity; raising questions to ensure that there is no underachievement within the school.

With greater emphasis on inclusivity and underachievement (as opposed to attainment) this guidance acts as a prompt to crystallise the school's thinking on monitoring. It reminds the senior management team and subject coordinators/leaders about the rich variety of pupil groupings within the school and raises some key questions.

Links to school cycle

This guidance can be introduced at the beginning of a new school year to ensure all categories of pupil groupings are identified. All data, including key stage tests, ongoing teacher assessment, in-house tests, attendance records, etc. to be linked with the relevant groupings throughout the year.

Key personnel

Senior management and subject coordinators can use this guidance to ensure their monitoring is covering all pupil groupings. The groupings are not exhaustive and some will not be relevant to all schools. Senior management should decide what specific groupings should have top priority for their own school monitoring.

How this contributes to school improvement

Encouraging key personnel to focus on inclusivity and achievement in their own school, a key Ofsted focus.

- Promotes discussion (and therefore greater awareness) between all staff on pupil groupings within the school.
- More focused monitoring.

Next steps

See 'Whole-school monitoring' proforma (3).

This proforma can be used for whole-school monitoring and has further guidance notes.

(2) Monitoring basic skills with inclusivity in mind

We aim to be 'all-inclusive' with regard to educational and social experiences at our school. We celebrate our differences but endeavour to ensure that our variety of backgrounds, situations and circumstances do not lead to individual or groups of pupils underachieving. In short, our aim is to ensure that every child and adult at our school achieves to their full potential in all aspects of their school life.

The following is not an exhaustive list but begins to identify the rich variety of individuals/groups within our school context.

The differences can be as a result of:

- race, gender, special educational needs (including gifted pupils), social/economic background or culture.

There may also be the following categories of pupils/adults within our school:

- those with English as an additional/second language and/or from an ethnic minority background
- those with a disability
- those children in public care or who are young carers
- those who are categorised as travellers or gypsies.

There can, of course, be a combination of the above categories for individuals or groups of children/adults

Ongoing key questions:

- How do standards of achievement compare between the above individuals and groups?
- Is there evidence of underachievement with any individual or group?
- What strategies are being employed to redress the balance?

See: 'Whole-school monitoring' proforma (3).

Proforma 3: Whole-school monitoring

Objective
To record the pupil groupings on a standardised form and highlight other key data about the grouping, so enabling an informative grouping profile to emerge.

The second part of this form is for guidance and can be used as a valuable *aide-mémoire* as well as assisting in identifying the definitive cohort to be monitored.

Links to school cycle
You may decide to incorporate this proforma at the beginning of the school year, as a result of a looming inspection or as a response to data that has identified underachievement with a specific cohort of pupils. On the other hand you may simply wish to use it as a starting point for a staff discussion on monitoring and inclusivity.

Key personnel
Senior management team and subject coordinators for whole-school monitoring.

How this contributes to school improvement
- Ensures monitoring of all groups of pupils in the school.
- Provides an *aide-mémoire* for developing cohort profile and evaluating the work.

Next steps
Ensure all information is passed on to appropriate senior managers, including the special needs coordinator.

After evaluating data and cohort profile, give some thought to whether there are some overlaps with other school groups. For example, is a large proportion of summer-born boys on the SEN register? Are they all British white or are they made up of varying ethnic groups? Conversely, is the higher attaining group made up of autumn-born British white girls?

(3) Whole-school monitoring – focus group proforma

Number of pupils at this school:	
Focus group:	Date:
Percentage whole-school terms:	Number:
Percentage on SEN register:	Number:
Percentage on statements:	Number:
Initials or other identification of focus group/classes:	
Related curriculum targets:	
Notes including review date:	

Evaluating pupils' work

Selecting pupils' work for scrutiny and/or tracing different individuals/cohorts.

Considerations

- **What individuals/cohort do you wish to sample?**

- **Inclusion:** Consider collecting work by different groups.
  (Boys/girls; above average, average and below average; SEN; EAL; age; key stage; different ethnic backgrounds; gifted/talented; social/economic groups; month of birth; pupils with disabilities; pupils in public care and pupils who are carers.)

- **Progress:** The sample should enable you to come to a judgement about progress/improvement over time, so you will need to access work over a period of weeks or across terms/years.

- **Context:** You should be able to place the work in the context of:
  - the syllabus
  - the teacher's planning
  - expected standards/National Curriculum levels.

- **Pupils:** You can learn a lot about standards, and progress in particular, by talking to pupils about the work you have selected. They can give you an indication of how they think they have improved and why.

Proforma 4: Work sampling

Objective

To conduct effective work sampling by scrutinising samples of the work of pupils working at above average, average and below average levels.

The prompt questions and guidance will help to gain a greater insight into the pupils' attitudes to learning, understanding and ability.

Links to school cycle

This proforma can be used throughout the year by a member of the senior management team or subject coordinator/leader while carrying out their monitoring duties.

The questions can also be used by a teacher or teaching assistant to gauge individual, groups or whole-class perceptions, regarding their learning experiences.

Alternatively a school governor might be deployed to ask such questions and give feedback to the relevant staff.

Key personnel

- Senior management team
- Subject coordinator
- Teacher
- Governor

How this contributes to school improvement

Ofsted has found discussing work with pupils to be a very powerful inspection tool. It gives a first-hand insight into teaching and learning, especially when the discussion centres on the pupils' completed work.

If senior managers and subject coordinators ensure this strategy is embedded within their own practice, greater awareness of insights into teaching and learning at the school are likely to emerge.

Next steps

Use the information to feed back to relevant personnel. In future monitoring, ensure existing strengths are built upon and there is improvement in areas that were causing concern.

(4) Work sampling

Three pupils from appropriate class/es working at above average standard, average standard, below average standard and any other relevant category should bring work with them.

General questions might include:

- What did you really enjoy doing?

- Why?

- Tell me about some of the things that you have learned.

- How do you think you are getting on in...?

- What didn't you enjoy doing?

- What things did you find most difficult?

- Why? Etc.

Focus also on specific pieces of work and ask them to tell you about how/why/when they did it, etc.

Other possible questions

Proforma 5: Subject report evaluation sheet

Objective

To obtain a written subject report from a pupil's perspective and additional personal information through interaction with the pupil.

Links to school cycle

This proforma can be used as an evaluation tool after a section/module of work and/or to provide supplementary information for end-of-year reports.

Teachers and subject coordinators could also give a specific cohort and/or whole year group the first part of the proforma to fill out in order to get an instant overview of the pupils' collective learning.

Key personnel
- Subject coordinators
- Teachers

How this contributes to school improvement
- Provides informative feedback for teachers and subject coordinators that can assist with teaching/learning/curriculum evaluation.
- Highlights any inconsistencies between achievement and attitude.

The pupils' attitude towards learning plays an important part in the process of an Ofsted inspection.

Next steps
- Pass on the information to the relevant members of staff.
- Ensure description of completed work is consistent with the school's programme of study.
- Log the attitude and other personal grades for future monitoring to see if there is an upward or downward trend.

(5) Subject report evaluation sheet – pupil's perspective

Subject .... Year ....

Term .... Name ....

I have completed some work on

I have learned

Other comments

Adult evaluation after discussion with pupils

	Poor				Excellent
Attitude	1	2	3	4	5
Confidence	1	2	3	4	5
Motivation	1	2	3	4	5
Attention	1	2	3	4	5
Applying subject?	1	2	3	4	5

(only grade if appropriate)

Proforma 6: Class survey

Objective

To gauge the pupils' responses before the official letters and/or questionnaires are sent out at the time of the next Ofsted inspection.

To familiarise and clarify meaning for pupils so they can answer future questions more confidently.

To give valuable feedback for the class teacher.

Links to school cycle

As the above indicates this would be a useful preliminary exercise before the official Ofsted inspection. It can also provide the class teacher with an insight into how individuals, groups or even the whole class is feeling. Completing them towards the end of each term might prove useful and enable the teacher to gauge upward and downward trends in pupils' perceptions. Over a longer term (two to three years) it would be fascinating to compare results.

Key personnel

- Class teacher

How this contributes to school improvement

If Ofsted finds similar information useful, then it is certainly helpful to class teachers by:

- giving valuable insight into how pupils view the class ethos and organisation
- encouraging the teacher to take stock and celebrate what they are doing well: success breeds success
- ensuring the teacher has no 'blind spots' and is presented with areas that might need improving.

Next steps

The teacher reflects on both strengths and points to develop and notes them on proformas 21–22 (prompting sentences proformas) as appropriate.

(6) Class survey

We are going to conduct our own class survey. Please answer all questions honestly. Please don't write only what you think teachers want to hear. Your answers could be different from your friends'.

	Yes	Don't know	No
I am happy to be in my class			
I know what the learning objectives are for most lessons			
I enjoy coming to school			
My teacher enjoys teaching			
I think my school rules are fair			
There is usually an adult to help me when I'm stuck			
I feel safe at school			
I am always expected to work hard in class			
There is always a helpful adult to talk to at school			
Most of my class concentrate on their work			
I know my target/s			
I know what to do to achieve my targets			
My teacher usually has time for me			
Homework helps my learning			
My work is usually marked			
We always celebrate good work in class			
I know a little about the different ways children learn			
All the children in my class get on with each other			
All the children in my school usually get on with each other			
My class is usually an exciting place to learn in			
My time at school usually goes by quickly			
My parents/carers know how to help me with school work			
I enjoy playtimes and dinnertimes			
I enjoy the school assemblies			

The best thing about my school is
_____
_____

My school would be better if
_____
_____

Proforma 7: Expectation sheet

Objective
To provide a class/year group expectation profile very quickly from which future target-setting data can be produced.

Links to school cycle
A whole-school audit can take place using this proforma to evaluate how different year groups are progressing. This can be another source of information prior to setting pupil targets. This sheet can also cover individual subjects, especially for literacy and numeracy targets.

The proformas can be completed by using pupils' initials and/or straightforward numbers. The only pupils who are not recorded are those working at or above the expected level. This proforma is particularly useful in identifying pupils who are slightly below the expected level, where a minimal increase of resources might have a big impact on overall attainment.

The information on this proforma can be used in conjunction with proforma 9, 'SATs predictions'.

Key personnel
- Senior management team
- Subject coordinators
- Teachers

How this contributes to school improvement
The simplicity of this proforma enables the relevant personnel to see at an instant how a cohort of pupils is progressing without having to wade through a large amount of numerical data.

This enables appropriate personnel to make quick and informal decisions about future strategies and the targets of resources.

The proforma can provide valuable monitoring/tracking information for senior managers if it is completed on a regular termly/yearly cycle.

The above approach will ensure that the school has qualitative information on which to base realistic but challenging pupil targets. Such an approach will provide quality evaluative data for Ofsted.

Next steps
By calculating the percentage of pupils who are not included on the proforma (because they are at or above the expected level) you are left with the percentage that are below the expected level. Similarly if you include those pupils who are only 'slightly below' those at or above the expected level you can assess how significant such an upward shift would be to school statistics. This information will be very useful to the senior management team.

(7) Expectation sheet

Class .... Year ....

Children working below their expected level in   (subject)
a)   Slightly below
b)   Below
c)   Substantially below
Strategies to counter underachievement
No. in class   Usual time of lesson
Calculations
If A achieve   =
If B achieve   =
If C achieve   =

Optimus Education

Proforma 8: Attitude/progress sheet

Objective

To provide an instant pupil profile snapshot covering effort, achievement and personal information.

Links to school cycle

This proforma provides supplementary information for the school's termly or annual report. It can also be used as part of the school's routine monitoring on groups of pupils.

The collation of both personal attributes and academic progress can be valuable information for the school and Ofsted's inclusive agenda.

Key personnel

- Senior management team
- Subject coordinator
- Teacher

How this contributes to school improvement

This form can highlight anomalies in effort and achievement. For example, if a pupil is achieving at B and only scores C for effort, questions might be asked about the pupil's lack of motivation and how to improve effort so as to increase performance.

Other personal attributes can also be assessed and pupils with similar profiles, for instance those who score low with their listening skills, might be placed on an in-house development programme.

Next steps

Look for potential correlations in the data, for example, between low achievement and poor listening scores, or between low achievement and poor communication skills and so on.

Using these forms at regular intervals might highlight, for example, that moving from a steady to improving trend is often accompanied by a significant improvement in one or more of the personal attributes scores. This information, set in the context of your own school, will be extremely useful to the appropriate personnel.

(8) Attitude/progress sheet

Subject .... Year ....

Date .... Name ....

	Poor				Excellent
Confidence	1	2	3	4	5
Motivation	1	2	3	4	5
Listening	1	2	3	4	5
Communication	1	2	3	4	5

Effort	Achievement	Trend
A	A	**Improving**
B	B	
C	C	**Steady**
D	D	
E	E	**More application needed**

Comments

Proforma 9: SATs predictions

Objective
To provide an instant snapshot (best and worst case scenarios) for SATs predictions in English, mathematics and science.

To highlight where related information can be found.

Links to school cycle
This proforma can be incorporated at any time during the school year. It gives the senior management team and teacher a clear overview of SATs predictions. There is no need to wait until the actual year of the SATs to complete this form; using it in the preceding year/s can highlight strengths and weaknesses.

The information on this proforma can be used in conjunction with the 'Expectation sheet' proforma (7).

Key personnel
- Senior management team
- Subject coordinators
- Teacher

How this contributes to school improvement
If the proforma is incorporated as a regular part of school monitoring and well before the SATs period, it can highlight areas that may need attention and leave a realistic timescale to take appropriate action. If it is used in conjunction with 'Expectation sheet' proforma (7), the senior management team gain further detail and greater insight into the overall situation.

Next steps
Start to cross-reference the 'related information' in order to gain an accurate and realistic year group profile.

Review 'Expectation sheet' proforma (7) and reconsider whether your predictions are too cautionary or optimistic.

Improving Performance in Primary Schools

Proformas 1-9

(9) SATs predictions

Name of teacher (current and previous)		
Year 2 SATs	Year 6 SATs	Results:
Percentage achieving level .... in		

Subject	Best case scenario	Worst case scenario
English		
Mathematics		
Science		

Related information	
No. IEPs	
Previous: QCA optional SATs results	
Relevant in-house test information	
Teacher assessment/evidence	
Baseline assessment or otherwise	

Comments

Optimus Education

Proformas 10-14

Assisting the subject coordinators in their role

Proforma 10: Subject coordinators' checklist

Objective

To provide the subject coordinators with a checklist to help prioritise their tasks.

Links to school cycle

The school improvement plan will dictate the tasks that are currently most/least important. In addition there may be some subjects that are left on the back-burner for a while because they have had recent scrutiny and/or others have been given a high priority through the school's own self-evaluation or through other external agencies, such as Ofsted.

Key personnel

- Senior management team
- Subject coordinators

How this contributes to school improvement

The form identifies key tasks that effective schools should carry out. They are not exhaustive, but if they are being covered in all subjects within a given time frame it is almost definite that school improvement is taking place on a broad scale.

Next steps

Many of the tasks correlate with proformas in the coordinators, monitoring, performance management and whole-school development sections; the permutations are too numerous to list here.

A good starting point, in consultation with your line manager, would be to select the appropriate proformas from the overall pack in order to gauge the breadth and depth of the tasks over a short-, medium- and long-term perspective.

(10) Subject coordinators' checklist

Name	Date	Subject/focus
Compiling/updating portfolio		
Check planning and its links to learning		
Team teaching		
Lesson observation		
Policy review		
Reviewing/ordering resources		
Evaluate standards/achievements		
Course attendance		
Leading colleagues		
Organising INSET		
Promoting cross-curricular links		
Liaising parent/governors		
Monitor pupils' work		
Activity relating to raising standards		
Specific knowledge update		
Other		

Notes

Proforma 11: Subject coordinators' summary of monitoring

Objective

To assist the coordinator in gaining an overview of what monitoring proformas are available and their reference numbers.

Links to school cycle

Monitoring pupils' work has always been an important part of the subject coordinator's role.

The school development plan should highlight which subjects have been given the highest priority and which aspects of the subject need attention.

This is likely to dictate the monitoring focus and future strategy.

Key personnel
- School management team
- Subject coordinators

How this contributes to school improvement

Whole-school monitoring is a broad description that on the one hand can seem too vast for one person to manage, yet on the other hand too vague and general to have a specific impact on school improvement.

The proformas assist the subject coordinator in dealing with this uncertainty by breaking up monitoring into several strands. The proformas will assist with school improvement because they are streamlined, focused, easy to use and will provide specific information that can be evaluated to inform future progress.

Next steps

Share all monitoring information with your line manager and other coordinators at appropriate times. It can be very informative to see how individuals and groups of pupils perform in different subjects.

Their attitude towards different subjects may also raise interesting questions. Does monitoring indicate that pupils have strengths and weaknesses/likes/dislikes in different subjects, or is it also to do with the teaching of such subjects?

(11) Subject coordinators' summary of monitoring

Activity:	Proforma numbers	Action taken/date
Marking of pupils' work	1	
Monitoring of inclusivity	2	
Evaluating pupils' work	3, 4, 5 and 8	
Evaluating pupils' attitudes	6 and 8	
Evaluating future standards	7 and 9	
Other information		

Proforma 12: Improving standards

Objective
To provide a framework for a subject coordinator to write a report about standards in their subject.

All too often subject reports are too general, this guidance ensures the report focuses on standards and achievement.

Links to school cycle
See 'Subject coordinators' summary of monitoring' proforma (11).

Proforma 11 can direct the coordinator to specific proformas that will assist with this report on standards.

Key personnel
- Subject coordinators

How this contributes to school improvement
The framework of this proforma ensures the focus is on standards/achievement and because of this it does not become a general unfocused report.

Two sections of the report specifically cover how development work has improved standards and how future development work will improve standards in the future.

Next steps
Share the report with your line manager.

Reflect whether development work carried out to improve standards in your own subject could be transferred to other areas of the curriculum in order to spread the improvement to other subjects.

(12) Improving standards

Improving standards in .... (subject)

Brief report

Current standards/achievement (including specific cohorts of pupils year/key stage groups, etc.)

Recent development work and how this has improved standards

Future development work and how this will improve standards

Other comments

Proforma 13: Self-appraisal for subject coordinators

Objective

To assist a subject coordinator in evaluating and reflecting on their current and future role/s.

Links to school cycle

The ideal time to complete this proforma is prior to a performance management interview with a line manager.

Key personnel

- Subject coordinator

How this contributes to school improvement

This ensures that the subject coordinator's responsibilities and aspirations are not overlooked by their line manager. Information on this proforma may highlight future possibilities that the line manager had not considered. Whenever practicable, if information on this sheet is acted upon in a positive way, staff are more likely to feel valued, resulting in a likely increase in both motivation and performance.

Next steps

Whenever possible these proformas should be considered collectively because if acted upon, each individual outcome will have a knock-on effect on overall staffing responsibilities.

(13) Self-appraisal for subject coordinators

Name ....

Current responsibilities/subject

Responsibilities/subjects prepared to take on

Extra-curricular offerings

Other comments

Proforma 14: My personal development planning sheet

Objective
To assist the member of staff in devising their own personal development plan.

Links to school cycle
This is likely to be completed after or during a performance management interview with line manager.

Key personnel
- Teacher
- Subject coordinator
- Senior management team

How this contributes to school improvement
This proforma assists with personal/professional development.

Developing and investing in staff is an integral part of school improvement not least because it will unlock staff potential and increase individual performance.

Next steps
Line managers should regularly scan these proformas and take note of the various headings to ensure that the plan remains dynamic.

For example, at any time during planning ask such questions as:

- Is progress to date, within the overall timescale, sufficient?
- Are appropriate resources being made available?
- Do the personnel identified as supporting this plan have sufficient experience, expertise and the personal qualities required?

(14) My personal development planning sheet

Priority

Target

Success criteria

Tasks

Time scale

Personnel to support me

Resources I will need

Monitoring review – how/who?

Evaluation

Miscellaneous notes

Proformas 15-20

Whole-school strategic planning

Proforma 15: Strategies for monitoring educational standards

Objective

To give the sequence and overview of key tasks associated with key tools for school improvement.

The list is not exhaustive but simply an *aide-mémoire* for starting points in school improvement work.

Links to school cycle

It is likely that the previous teaching/learning and/or subject coordinator proformas have already identified the issues and the way forward for you and your team.

However you arrived at your decision, once the tasks and tools have been decided upon, ensure you communicate all key aspects to the appropriate audiences. The last section of proforma 15 reminds you of opportunities for doing this.

Proforma 20, entitled 'School development', is a useful proforma to communicate and action whole-school planning.

Key personnel
- Senior management team
- Subject coordinators

How this contributes to school improvement

Assists the senior management team in strategic thinking while ensuring joined-up thinking and effective communication with a variety of stakeholders.

Next steps

Once decisions have been made about the sequence of key tasks and associated tools to be employed, thought should be given about staff/governor meeting airtime, use of professional development days and, if appropriate, what issues should be communicated to parents.

(15) Strategies for monitoring educational standards

Key tasks

- Identify the subject/s in which the school needs to improve
- Analyse the areas/aspects causing concern
- Ascertain whether a whole-school/key stage/year group problem
- Develop curriculum targets and related success criteria
- Prioritise key objectives
- Identify key personnel
- Evaluate resources available
- Implement monitoring and evaluation strategies.

Key tools

- Senior management team
- In-house monitoring data
- Other schools
- PANDA
- Autumn package
- SATs results (including optional and other tests)
- Baseline data
- Exemplification booklets
- Pupils' work (including prior attainment); category of pupil
- Robust planning/assessment, marking and monitoring policies/procedures.

Essential link-ups to enhance joined-up thinking and communicate goals/visions

- School development plan/Standards fund
- Performance management policy/procedures
- Whole-school staff meetings
- Governor meetings/working parties
- Parents' meetings/newsletters/assemblies
- Community: newspapers/school brochure.

Proforma 16: Subject priorities

Objective
To give an overview of subject teaching observations and the monitoring of work.

Links to school cycle
This proforma enables the senior management team to gain a clear overview of the tasks covered by the subject coordinator/leader. There may be valid reasons why some subjects have not been highlighted on this form. Remember, subject coordinators and their line managers may have referred to proformas 10–14 in order to prioritise or reprioritise work on specific subjects.

Key personnel
- Senior management team

How this contributes to school improvement
This proforma highlights gaps in teaching observations and work monitoring in different subject areas, thus ensuring no subjects are overlooked. If there are gaps, it is because of the school's priorities and not due to an oversight.

Next steps
If there are gaps in subject areas, ensure it is due to the planned priorities and discuss the gaps with the appropriate personnel.

(16) Subject priorities

Subject	Teaching observed	Work monitored (Year group)	Next steps
English			
Mathematics			
Science			
ICT			
RE			
PSHE			
History			
Geography			
Music			
Art			
D & T			
PE			

Proforma 17: Teacher appraisal/monitoring

Objective

To assist the senior management team with the monitoring of individual teacher appraisal.

This sheet is designed to be an ongoing summary record of appraisal for individual teachers.

Links to school cycle

Information for this proforma can be lifted from the relevant teaching and learning proformas 1–9 and subject coordinator proformas 10–14.

Key personnel

- Senior management team
- Head

How this contributes to school improvement

This proforma encourages the appraisal process to be ongoing as opposed to a one-off event. Continual development in small regular steps is more likely to have a greater impact on staff/school improvement than an annual or bi-annual snapshot of performance.

The final section of the proforma is completed by both parties in discussion with the head, so that the appraisal process itself can be monitored in order to ensure its ongoing effectiveness.

Next steps

Review the proforma in conjunction with the relevant teaching and learning proformas 1–9 and/or subject coordinator proformas 10–14. Proforma 14, 'My personal development planning sheet', may be particularly useful.

(17) Teacher appraisal/monitoring

Name .... Date ....

The teacher: Classroom practice	
• Demonstrates and applies effective teaching/learning with all pupils including differentiated work with a whole class, group and individual pupils (See Ofsted/literacy/numeracy lesson observation proformas).	**1 2 3 4 5 6**
• Readily identifies issues that need addressing.	**1 2 3 4 5 6**
• Demonstrates ability to plan, organise and implement necessary action.	**1 2 3 4 5 6**
• Able to review progress based on appropriate and accurate data.	**1 2 3 4 5 6**
• The class is orderly and disciplined with a purposeful atmosphere.	**1 2 3 4 5 6**
• Other adults are being used effectively.	**1 2 3 4 5 6**

Appraiser comment

Pupils' work	
• Work handed in is of a reasonable/high standard and completed.	**1 2 3 4 5 6**
• Marking is consistent with productive feedback when appropriate.	**1 2 3 4 5 6**
• The presentation is of a good standard.	**1 2 3 4 5 6**
• Work is at the expected standard or above.	**1 2 3 4 5 6**
• Work covers appropriate National Curriculum programmes of study.	**1 2 3 4 5 6**
• Homework is used effectively to raise standards and is consistent with the school policy.	**1 2 3 4 5 6**

Appraiser comment

Other professional aspects	
• Good understanding of own subject/specialism.	**1 2 3 4 5 6**
• Work is well planned.	**1 2 3 4 5 6**
• The teacher ensures he/she has ongoing professional development.	**1 2 3 4 5 6**
• The teacher is seen as a support for colleagues.	**1 2 3 4 5 6**

Appraiser comment

To be completed with head	
Appraisal must:	
• Affect classroom practice in a positive way.	**1 2 3 4 5 6**
• Be manageable/minimal paperwork.	**1 2 3 4 5 6**
• Seen to be worth the effort by both parties.	**1 2 3 4 5 6**
• Be ongoing.	**1 2 3 4 5 6**

Rating 1 = Excellent, 6 = Poor

Proforma 18: Teaching and learning observations

Objective
To help the lesson observer focus on key questions that relate to effective teaching and learning.

Links to school cycle
Information could be transferred to the 'Teacher appraisal/monitoring' (17), 'Subject priorities' (16) or 'My personal development planning sheet' (14) proformas.

Key personnel
- Senior management team.

How this contributes to school improvement
Teaching and learning is at the heart of school improvement and this proforma ensures this is the focus. It is useful to give a copy of this proforma to those being observed so they can reflect on their own practice before the actual observations.

Next steps
See above links.

Rehearse the feedback session using the questions as prompts. Your lesson observation feedback should be to the point, clear and backed up by evidence. It is useful to highlight:
- what went well and why this was so
- what could be better and how this might be achieved.

If there are any real concerns then a dialogue with the appropriate personnel may need to take place. You may suggest that the observed teacher completes 'My personal development planning sheet' proforma (14) with you.

(18) Teaching and learning observations

- What are the lesson objectives?
- Has the teacher made the objectives clear from the outset?
- Are the lesson objectives appropriate for all pupils?
- Have appropriate resources been developed and made accessible to pupils?
- Does the teaching methodology cater for the range of individuals within the group?
- Is ICT being effectively incorporated into the lesson?
- Is appropriate differentiation incorporated?
- Are all pupils treated equally and included throughout the lessons?
- Are pupils engaged?
- Are pupils sufficiently challenged?
- Do they understand what is expected of them?
- Are they learning?
- Is the lesson well organised?
- Are other adults being deployed effectively?

After the lesson, through observation, talking to pupils and scrutinising work, ask yourself the following questions

- Have the learning objectives been met by all (almost all) pupils?
- Was this lesson unsatisfactory? Why?
- Was this lesson satisfactory? Why?
- Was this lesson good? Why?
- Was this lesson very good/excellent? Why?

Give at least two clear reasons for the above judgements, including two reasons why it didn't make the next grade

Proforma 19: Governing body

Objective
To enable governors (or other stakeholders) to get to the core of a problem before raising it as a vague concern at a school meeting.

Links to school cycle
This form can be used throughout the year and/or leading up to formal meetings where problems/concerns are discussed. If, having got to the core of the problem, a decision is made to add it to the school improvement plans, then the starting point would be the 'School development' proforma (20).

Key personnel
- Senior management team
- Governors
- Other stakeholders

How this contributes to school improvement
The proforma not only enables those adopting it to get to the core issues more quickly but saves a great deal of preliminary discussion, which often finds key stakeholders going round in circles.

The time and energy saved using this proforma allows for more focus on the central issues of school improvement.

Next steps
If the issue is deemed worthy of further investigation, transfer information to 'School development' proforma (20).

(19) Governing body

Dealing with issues in school

What is the problem?

Why is it a problem?

Evidence that the problem exists.

What do I suggest we do about the problem?

Agreed action after consultation with headteacher.

Does it need to be raised at a governors' meeting?

Yes? Please see chair at least three days before meeting.

Proforma 20: School development

Objective
The central proforma for all priorities which links the others together.

A common format on which to record all development areas/issues/concerns that are to emerge as the ongoing school improvement plan.

Links to school cycle
The different boxes can be cross-referenced to the appropriate heading on other proformas. For example, if the teaching of a specific subject is identified as a particular weakness, this might be cross-referenced to the 'Subject coordinators' checklist' (10), 'Improving standards' (12), 'Subject priorities' (16) and so on. Such proformas may or may not confirm that such weaknesses exist.

Key personnel
Any stakeholders who are entrusted by the senior management team or governors to have input into the school improvement plans.

How this contributes to school improvement
A well constructed proforma will give a clear direction in all aspects of school improvement.

The advantage of using loose leaf proformas is that they are easily duplicated and key personnel can have instant access to them.

In addition, unlike school improvement folders or documents, all aspects of school improvement can be worked on, updated and cross-referenced simultaneously and with ease.

Next steps
Collate all 'School development' proformas, proforma (20) and prioritise in categories A, B and C.

A = Action

B = Brewing

C = Coming up.

(20) School development

Priority

Target

Success criteria

Task/s

Timescale	**Personnel**	**Resources**
Monitoring and review	**Evaluation**	**Miscellaneous notes**

Proformas 21-24

Collating performance information

Proformas 21 and 22: Prompting sentences

Objective

Prompting sentences/alternative prompting.

To encourage a constructive performance management dialogue by suggesting prompt statements/questions.

Links to school cycle

Numerous proformas can be used in the above dialogue. Part of the preliminary discussions will centre on which proformas to incorporate in order to achieve a constructive and balanced dialogue.

Key personnel
- Senior management team
- Teacher

How this contributes to school improvement

Ensures a well balanced and fluid discussion based on evidence via the proformas. This should contribute to constructive outcomes which should have a positive effect on school improvement.

Next steps

Consider completing 'My personal development planning sheet' proforma (14).

(21) Prompting sentences – Sheet 1

1. I feel my greatest strength as a teacher is…

2. I am happiest in my work when…

3. The aspect of my work I have been most pleased about this year is…

4. I feel my most significant contribution to the school this year has been…

5. I feel my greatest weakness as a teacher is…

6. I feel the children I teach would benefit more from what I do if…

7. I feel the least successful aspect of my work over the last year has been…

8. My main targets for next year are…

9. The help I most need from the school is…

10. In two years' time, I see myself…

11. In ten years' time, I see myself…

12. I love teaching because…

(22) Alternative prompting – Sheet 2

1. Which aspects of your work do you feel especially pleased with?

2. Which aspects of your work have not gone as well as you might have hoped?

3. Are there any constraints or difficulties you are working under?

4. In what ways do you want to develop your work in the coming year?

5. What training or new skills do you think you need in the coming year?

Proforma 23: Continuous professional development for teachers

Objective

To provide 20 key questions for self-assessment/professional development that gets to the heart of teaching and learning.

The questions were selected after reflecting on effective practice based on research and evidence.

Links to school cycle

The questions may highlight gaps in practice and/or professional development and these can be noted on other proformas such as 'My personal development planning sheet' proforma (14).

Key personnel
- Senior management team
- Teachers

How this contributes to school improvement

The 20 questions encourage self-evaluation; as with school self-evaluation, this is an integral part of the improvement process.

Next steps
- Highlight priorities for improving practice.
- Highlight gaps in training and development.
- Try to ensure practice priorities and development complement each other.

(23) Continuous professional development for teachers

The 20 definitive questions regarding

- performance management/appraisal
- Ofsted
- threshold assessment.

1. Are you aware how you use body language in your teaching? Stillness, gestures, mannerisms, movement/relaxed posture, etc.
2. Are you aware how you use voice in your teaching? (Volume, pace, tone.)
3. Are you aware of your questioning style and techniques?
4. Are your expectations appropriate and challenging?
5. How do you ensure your own subject knowledge is secure?
6. Is your planning sound, purposeful and clear?
7. What use do you make of prior learning experiences/data?
8. Are you clear about what completed work should look like?
9. Is your teaching and assessment differentiated and focused?
10. Is your marking specific and informative?
11. Is your feedback directional?
12. Do you use objectives/targets to motivate the pupils?
13. Do you use homework as a natural back-up/progression to class work?
14. Is your class organised and set up to maximise teaching and learning?
15. How do you deploy your classroom assistant to ensure maximum benefits?
16. How do you make optimal use of educational resources?
17. How do you greet your class in the mornings, returning from break/lunchtime?
18. What strategy do you incorporate/adopt to ensure continuous professional development?
19. How do you support your colleagues?
20. What other questions do you need to ask in order to challenge your performance?

Proforma 24: Summary of CPD for individual teachers

Objective

To provide a summary of professional development for individual teachers.

Links to school cycle

The proforma should provide supplementary information for the performance management dialogue.

Key personnel
- Senior management team
- Teachers

How this contributes to school improvement

The summary of professional development will enable the teacher and school management team to highlight any gaps in the teachers' development/training, ensuring that all teachers receive a broad and balanced development programme. Effective and balanced professional development is more likely to enhance school improvement.

Next steps

Copies of these forms, completed by individual teachers, will be handed to the head so that he or she can monitor professional development of the whole staff.

- Highlight priorities for improving practice.
- Highlight gaps in training and development.
- Try to ensure practice priorities and development complement each other.

(24) Summary of CPD for individual teachers

Initials	Subject/theme/topic	Dates

Proformas 25-27

Performance management

Proformas 25 and 27: Performance management

To assist with clear linkage between this publication and the latest performance management regulations please see over leaf.

i.   The review meeting

ii. The planning statement/s

iii. The objectives

The school should use this publication in conjunction with its own performance management policy (Sept 07) and its related pay policy.

(25) The review meeting

i. The review meeting

Below are some of the key areas that should be covered in this meeting.

Ensure all evidence/documents/data are at hand for this meeting including the relevant job description.

This is a two-way professional dialogue reflecting on the last performance cycle and looking forward to the next one. Issues that affected past performance (positive or negative) and which may also affect future performances are identified.

Planned support in the past is reviewed and future support is considered. Previous professional development is evaluated and future needs are discussed.

Judgements should focus on how far performance criteria have been met.

Looking to the future – key questions for the next cycle

What would you like to achieve within the context of whole school improvement?

What would you like to achieve within your professional/personal context?

How do you see your career developing over the next year/next five years?

See also Prompting sentences (Proforma (21))

Agree classroom observation date/s

Objectives should focus on school/professional priorities. They should be time bound, challenging but achievable. Some objectives may be achievable within the performance management cycle whilst others may require a longer time span, in which case clear progress benchmarks should be agreed from the outset.

(26) The planning statement/s

ii. Planning statement/s

Relating to the current cycle of performance management

Reviewer	Date
Reviewee	**Date**
Pay/Conditions Implications	**Date**

Signed Reviewer .... Signed Reviewee ....

Key Related Proformas

(12) Improving standards
(13) Self-appraisal for subject coordinators
(14) My personal development planning sheet
(17) Teacher appraisal/monitoring
(18) Teaching and learning observations
(20) School development
(21) Prompting sentences-sheet 1
(23) Continuous professional development for teachers
(24) Summary of CPD for individual teachers

(27) The objectives

iii. The objectives

Appraiser .... Appraisee .... Date ....

Objective	Success criteria
Time Scale	
Objective	Success criteria
Time Scale	
Objective	Success criteria
Time Scale	
Objective	Success criteria
Time Scale	

To identify:

- Resources/strategies
- Professional development
- Links to school improvement
- Other related issues

Further reading

The Mind Map Book, Tony Buzan, Barry Buzan.
GP Putnams, 1996.
ISBN 0452273226.

The Numbers Game: the use of assessment data in primary and secondary schools by Ofsted inspectors, K Hedger and D Jesson.
Centre for performance evaluation and resource management, University of York, 1999.
ISBN 0953629910.

Leading the Learning School, Colin Weatherley.
Network Education Press, 2000.
ISBN 1855390701.

Leadership and the One Minute Manager, K Blanchard, P Zigarri, D Zigarri.
Quill, 2000.
ISBN 0688163556.

The Power of Positive Thinking, Norman Vincent Peale.
Simon and Schuster, 2003.
ISBN 0743234804.

School Self-evaluation Guidance, Cambridgeshire LEA.
Cambridge County Council, 2003.
ISBN 1904452078.

Excellence and Enjoyment: Learning and teaching in the primary years. Assessment for learning.
DfES 2004. Ref DfES 0521-2004 G

Excellence and Enjoyment: Learning and teaching in the primary years. Continuing professional development.
DfES 2004. Ref DfES 0344-2004 G

Speaking, Listening, Learning: working with children in Key Stages 1 and 2.
DfES 2004. Ref. DfES 0163-2004

The Seven Habits of Highly Effective People, Stephen R Covey.
Simon and Schuster, 2005.
ISBN 0743268164.